FURY FOCUSED

OF FATES AND FURIES
BOOK 2

MELISSA HAAG

To my family,
Thank you for your support and patience during all the hours I
hid away in my office to get this written.

To the many people involved in the writing process with me,
Thanks for having my back. I sleep better because of all of you!

FURY FOCUSED

Life in Uttira isn't easy for Megan. Knowing what she is hasn't helped her control her temper, an unfortunate personality trait that might just keep her from graduating. Her mood swings don't bother her as much as the weird side effects that come with them. When things start to go up in flames around her, she knows she needs help controlling her abilities. But, the only person with the answers abandoned Megan in Uttira months ago.

Megan knows she must find her mother in the real world. However, the only way out of the magical barrier surrounding Uttira is with the mark of Mantirum. A mark she will only receive if she can manage to graduate from Girderon Academy. In order to start her search, Megan needs to learn to control her temper...or die trying.

CHAPTER ONE

IN THE COMPLETE SILENCE OF GIRDERON ACADEMY'S SECRET library, my brain wanted to explode. The text explaining the numerous different types of giants and how to distinguish them, although not helping, wasn't the sole reason for my imminent mental melt down. Too many thoughts whirled in my head. Too many to think straight.

Groaning, I absent-mindedly lifted my hands from the thick, old book and rubbed my face. The damn thing slammed shut and flew back to its place on the shelves.

"Are you kidding me?"

I stood to retrieve the book from its spot, yet again. The stupid return spell, which kept the library neat and prevented anyone from leaving with one of these precious, nonsensical tomes, was driving me as crazy as my thoughts about everything that had happened over the weekend.

Nothing had really changed since Trammer's death, except my thinking. The Council, which consisted of Adira, the Quills, Raiden, and a few others, had decided that, as a fury, I'd be the best candidate to watch over the remaining humans until a new liaison could be found. I hadn't considered the implications when I'd agreed, but after a weekend to think about it, the responsibility of being a liaison was starting to get to me. Look at how many had died since I'd gotten here. Everything in Uttira seemed to want a piece of humans. How was I going to stop that from happening?

On top of that weighing thought, I had Oanen and the promise he'd somehow twisted from me. What the hell had I been thinking? My previous, single attempt at a relationship had ended epically with my fist. The last thing I wanted to do was throat punch Oanen because of some weird fury fit of temper.

Fine, that wasn't even it. I knew, as a fury, I only punished the wicked, and Oanen was far from wicked. He was great. Perfect. And, I was terrified of screwing it up with him. How many guys really wanted to go out with a girl who had a flash temper and a tendency to hit first and ask questions later? Not counting Oanen, I felt pretty sure the answer would be none.

With the book once again in my hands, I returned to my uncomfortable seat at the old table and forced myself to focus as I started reading again. It wasn't easy. Because of the way the book had been added to by different people throughout the ages, it didn't read like a book but more like a recipe card with special notes.

Not all giants were giants by human standards. The term giant could describe the creature's size but also their birth place. Most giants mastered the ability to control their size by adolescence. Only a few had other gifts, in addition to having the magic to change their appearance. Most just trained as warriors in case the gods ever called upon them to once again fight in their wars over earth.

None of the information on the pages seemed particularly valuable. I sighed and scratched my forehead while keeping one hand firmly in the center of the book. From my place in the middle of the moderately-sized room, I looked up at the other volumes lining the shelves along the stone walls. Adira had suggested I pick a shelf and start reading the contents, in order, so I didn't miss anything. There were a lot of books. Over five hundred, at least. And if they all read like this one, I would just be wasting my time.

Rolling my shoulders, I got back to reading again and tried to ignore the doubts that kept poking at my mind.

A SUDDEN KNOCK on the thick, old door echoed in the room and made me jump. Not that the book I currently read was that gripping. I was just that focused on trying to absorb the words.

Standing, I realized how badly my back ached. I worked out the kink as I moved toward the door and wondered how long I'd been reading. Adira had taken my phone when I'd arrived, saying that entering with any kind of technology would just destroy the device due to a spell that prevented classified information from being copied and shared. All of which made no sense to me. One, there wasn't anything important in here as far as I'd read. And two, what was to stop me from just telling someone what I learned? But, I hadn't argued with her. Giving up my phone to hang out in a library and avoid sessions and other people had seemed a fair enough trade.

I opened the door, expecting to see Adira checking up on me like she'd said she would. Instead, I found Oanen leaning against the frame, his muscled arms crossed and his close-cropped, golden hair glinting in the light of the hall. My pulse gave a sudden jump at the sight of him. I still couldn't believe I'd said yes to being his girlfriend.

His blue gaze held mine, and a hint of a smile tugged at his lips.

"You look surprised," he said. "Expecting someone else?"

"Yeah. Adira. She said she'd check in on me."

"She mentioned that she did when I saw her in the hall. Both times you were reading."

"What? She never came in here."

"She doesn't need to with her portals," he said. "Come on. I figured you'd forget lunch if I didn't come get you." He straightened away from the door so I could step out.

"It's only lunch time?" I groaned. It felt like I'd spent the whole day in the library already.

He wrapped his arm around my shoulders as we walked.

"Yep. Only lunch. Three more hours of reading."

I barely heard what he'd said. My heart pounded in my ears as the feel of his arm around me sent my internal temperature from I'm-fine to is-it-hot-in-here.

His fingers idly stroked down my arm as he continued to speak.

"Don't worry. We'll do something fun afterwards to make up for it."

All sorts of warning buzzers started going off in my head. Fun? What did he mean by fun? Was that code for kissing? It was too soon for that, right? Before I could completely send myself into a full-blown panic, I spoke up. "You're freaking me out."

He sighed and dropped his arm.

"Yeah, I could tell by your pulse. I was wondering how long you'd let it go."

I turned on him and slugged him in the shoulder.

"That wasn't nice."

"No. It wasn't," he said. "And yet you didn't get fury angry, only girly mad."

I narrowed my eyes at him.

"Are you testing me?"

"No. I'm helping you see that I'm right and that there's nothing for you to worry about. You won't fly into a rage and hurt me."

He reached out and gently touched my cheek. My slowly calming pulse went right back to racing, and Oanen's lips quirked upward ever so slightly again.

"Not only do I make your heart race, I make you blush, too," he said softly. "I like it."

He wasn't making me just blush, he was turning my insides into molten lava. I stepped back, breaking the contact to gulp in some cooler air.

"You said slow. And I'm not even sure I'm ready for touching yet. So, keep your hands to yourself."

He tucked his hands into his front pockets and innocently arched a brow at me.

"That's a start." I resumed walking, and he stuck to my side as we navigated the busy halls toward the cafeteria.

"What did you bring for lunch?" he asked.

"Nothing. I figured I'd grab a tray."

Yet, even as I stepped into the cafeteria, I knew standing in line was a bad idea. At least one out of ten students was doing or thinking something to set off my fury to a mild degree. Individually, it wasn't enough to send me into a fit. Collectively, it was close.

"I packed an extra lunch if you'd rather skip the line," Oanen said when I hesitated.

"Yeah, that might be a better option."

We crossed the crowded cafeteria to get to the nearly vacant courtyard. Few students braved the cool fall air to lounge on the browning lawns and enjoy their lunches outdoors. Eliana already sat on a low wall near the trees.

As soon as she saw us, her face lit up with her usual shy smile, and she waved. I returned the wave, relieved she still seemed fine. Since she'd heard Trammer's insensitive remark about the creatures here being parasites that fed off of humans, I'd worried about her. She'd been sensitive about being a succubus before the man went on his hate rant.

"How'd the reading go?" she asked when I sat next to her. Oanen handed me one of the three insulated lunch bags she had nearby.

"It was okay. I was expecting some big secrets; instead, it's just—"

My lips kept moving but no sound came out.

"Part of the binding spell in the library," Oanen said. "You can't talk about what you read." He unwrapped his sandwich and took a large bite.

"Don't worry," Eliana said. "Anything that's common

knowledge will loosen up inside you after a few days, and you'll be able to talk about it. It's a different sort of spell. Tricky. And not often used because of its quirks."

She noticed my surprised look and paused.

"What?" she asked.

"How do you know all this? Have you been in the library already?" Adira had made it sound like letting students in there was something they normally don't do.

"No. I was stuck in beginner's magic two years ago. All any of the druid-types could talk about was the binding spell. Getting it right shows a level of mastery that only a few like Adira have." Eliana pointedly opened my bag, which sat in my lap, and handed me my sandwich. "It was a really long year."

I unwrapped my lunch and glanced at Oanen, who'd already finished the majority of his. Taking a bite, I paused at the flavor and looked at the sandwich.

"Do you like it?" Oanen asked.

I finished chewing and swallowed as I studied the peanut butter and marshmallow fluff interior.

"Yeah. It's different but good. What is it?"

"A chocolate fluffernutter sandwich. My mom remembered them from the sixties. Well, the regular fluffernutters. They didn't have chocolate peanut butter back then."

I took another bite, enjoying the sugary goodness. It hit the sweet craving I'd been having for weeks now.

"Eliana mentioned that you missed some of the food from outside. I thought this might help."

I looked at his remaining bite of the healthier turkey club he held.

"You didn't want one of these, too?"

His lips did that small little twitch thing again like he'd almost smiled.

"I'm saving the peanut butter for you."

The way he looked at me and the remembered feel of his hand on my arm sent my heart racing again.

"I see Jenna. I'm going to go say hi," Eliana said, quickly moving to leave me alone with Oanen.

I grabbed her arm and turned to her, my eyes wide and, probably, panicked.

"Now? I thought we were having lunch together."

She rolled her eyes at me and tugged her arm from my grasp.

"Yes. Sandwiches. Not the stuff you two are throwing off. I'll be back when you're calmer."

She hurried away. Flushed red with embarrassment and guilt, I stared at my sandwich.

"She's not mad," Oanen said. "She's afraid." He paused for a moment. "Like you."

I looked up at him.

"This doesn't need to be awkward," he said. "I like you. Your smile. The way you think. Your temper. All of it. I think that saying we're together is scaring you because you think it means something more than it should."

"What does it mean?"

"That we're spending more time together to get to know each other better."

"That's it?"

"For now? Yes."

Why did he have to go and say, "for now?" I wanted to groan and cover my face.

He leaned closer.

"I can hear your heart beating faster. 'Now' doesn't worry you, does it?"

I shook my head.

"Good. Then, eat your sandwich, Megan, and stop worrying about what comes later."

Forcing my thoughts to something other than the large, muscled Oanen who smelled like summer and wind and everything I wanted to inhale, I thought about the library and managed to calm down after a few more bites.

"I haven't found anything talking about the history of the gods. What can you tell me about them? I mean, they were real, I get that. But, why did they create all of us and then just leave?"

He stuffed his lunch containers back into his bag.

"I'm not sure that they just left. No one really knows what happened to them. They just stopped directing us."

"All at once? Like, maybe they all died?"

He shook his head. "Gods don't die. And I don't think it happened all at once. But again, no one really knows. It happened a long time ago. Some of us live very long lives, but I don't think anyone is that old. All we have are stories passed down from those who were there during that time. Stories that are probably in those books."

I groaned.

"The writing in those books is awful. Old. Hard to read."

"And I'm guessing not all in English."

"Dunno. I haven't made it very far," I admitted.

"Why are you asking about the gods?"

"Something I read. Not all of the creatures seem to have

strongly defined purposes without the gods here to tell them what to do."

"Yeah. That's part of why the Council and places like Uttira are necessary. It provides meaning for those without a purpose and accountability for those whose purposes don't align with the collective objective of remaining hidden from humans."

Eliana crossed the yard and rejoined us.

"You two all right now?" she asked, hesitating to sit.

"Yeah," I said quickly. Not wanting to think about what had sent her running, I continued the conversation with Oanen. "It still doesn't sit right with me, though. They created us, made us with these...instincts, then just bailed."

"That's the nature of things," Oanen said with a shrug.

I opened my bag of organic potato chips and munched, lost in thought while Eliana hurried to eat her lunch before the bell rang.

If we were keeping each other accountable, and creatures like me were keeping humans accountable, who was keeping the gods accountable?

CHAPTER TWO

"ALMOST DONE WITH THE FIRST BOOK OF GIANTS, I SEE."

I jumped slightly at the sound of Adira's voice and turned to give her a disgruntled look.

"First book? There's another book filled with useless giant information?"

She chuckled. "You might think it's useless now, but when you confront a giant for some misdeed you have discovered, what will your first thought be?"

"I'd wonder what race of giant it was. Mostly, if it's a magic using race that can manipulate time and space. The book makes those sound like the most dangerous."

"Or the most useful. What else would you consider?"

"If the giant is in its true form or if it gets bigger."

"And that information would help you decide how to deal with any wicked giant you encounter, yes?"

"I guess."

She set a hand on my shoulder.

"You're learning more than you know. Information and knowledge will only help you as you grow into your powers. And, in your role as temporary liaison. Which brings me to the reason why I've interrupted you before Oanen arrives. We're concerned about Ashlyn. Would you check on her after you leave here?"

"Sure."

A knock sounded on the door, and I glanced that direction, eager to escape the library. I looked back at Adira to see if she had anything else she needed me to do, but she was gone. Lifting my hand, I let the book fly back to its place on the shelf and hurried to make my escape.

"Ready?" Oanen asked when I opened the door.

"Yep. I've read more than I wanted to today."

I left the library, and the door shut softly behind me.

"Want to do something tonight?" he asked.

Why did I feel relieved that I had an excuse to say no?

"I can't. Adira asked me to go check on Ashlyn. Liaison duty, I guess." And, it was an official duty that I knew needed to be done. Since Ashlyn's uncle had killed himself, leaving her alone in Uttira, I'd wanted to talk to her. To make sure she was okay with her decision to stay.

"Okay. I'll drop you off there," Oanen said.

When we reached the student parking lot, Eliana's car was already gone.

"Are you sure Eliana isn't mad?" I asked, looking at Oanen.

"I told her not to wait. I drove a different car today."

"Oh, the hardships of your life. Not only do you need to decide what to wear each morning, you need to decide which car to drive." I rolled my eyes and followed him as he walked toward the back of the parking lot.

Amidst the gleaming reds, blues, and blacks sat a small

orange car. Although new and shiny, it lacked the pompous display of the sports cars that dominated the lot. I grinned when he went right to it.

"Slumming?" I asked.

His lips twitched, and he opened the door for me without a word.

Alone with Oanen for the first time since I'd woken up half sprawled on him, I wasn't sure what to do or say. Why did liking him have to feel so damn awkward?

Thankfully, it didn't take long for us to get to Ashlyn's house.

"I'm not sure how long I'll be," I said as he parked.

"Doesn't matter." He turned off the car.

"Are you sure you want to wait?" I asked.

"I don't plan to. I'll fly from here, and you can take your car home." He opened the door and got out.

Frowning, I hurried to do the same. He met me on the sidewalk near the front of the car.

"Wait. What do you mean? You're loaning me this car?"

"Sure."

I narrowed my eyes at Oanen, real annoyance rising.

"Half-truths and pacifying answers are just as good as lies. I don't do lies," I said.

"Fair enough. I don't do lies either. I do, however, like to do things that will likely annoy you."

"Such as?"

"Such as asking my parents to get you a car so you're not stuck waiting for a ride from someone. Especially when you're so far out of town."

"So your parents bought me a car?"

He remained silent while just looking at me, his arms crossed.

"I'm about to hit you," I warned.

"I purchased the car; they retrieved it."

"Boyfriends don't buy girlfriends cars," I said.

"The good ones do."

I breathed deeply, trying not to get angry with him.

"Since I fly and you don't, you need a car. Unless you're saying you like riding me?"

My mouth dropped open, and my heart started hammering again.

This time he flashed a grin large enough to show teeth.

"You're adorable," he said. "I could stand here and watch you blush all day, but neither of us will get anything done then."

He whipped off his shirt and tossed it to me. I caught it by reflex.

"What are you doing?" I demanded when he reached for his pants.

"Flying home. Keep the clothes in the car. It never hurts to have spares handy." He unzipped his fly, and I glanced at the houses lining the street.

"You can't be serious right now. You're standing on the sidewalk in the middle of the afternoon about to drop your pants for the world so you can turn into a griffin and fly away. What happened to keeping our presence secret?" I would have asked what happened to his modesty, but he'd never really had any from the start.

"If there was anyone new in Uttira, we would know. Anyone watching already knows about us. They'll just have to close their eyes if they don't want to see something."

I wondered if I should close my eyes, too. The problem was that I wanted to see Oanen in all his glory again. Badly. But that would likely result in more blushing. So, I compromised with myself and averted my gaze to the side. I could tell he was stepping out of his pants but couldn't see the details.

"Call me when you finish with your visit if you want some company," he said as he folded his clothes and set them on the car.

I nodded but didn't look at him until I heard the sound of his wings beating the air. With a deep calming breath, I turned and went to the house. I couldn't believe it had only been a few days since I'd last been there.

Ashlyn opened the door after my third knock, her hazel eyes bloodshot and puffy. The mottled complexion of her pale skin made her neatly brushed, strawberry-blonde hair seem even more red.

"Ashlyn, I'm so sorry," I said. Anger and regret welled up inside me. The normal, non-fury kind. "I know we don't know each other well, but would you like some company for a while?"

She nodded. "Adira mentioned you'd probably stop by."

I stepped into her house. Her home seemed so oddly normal given what her uncle, Trammer, had done.

"Can I get you something to drink?" she asked politely as she closed the door.

"No, thank you."

She led the way to the living room and took a seat on the couch. I wasn't sure what to say or do, so I looked around the room while I gave myself a moment to think.

The book I'd last seen her reading sat on the nearby coffee table.

"It's a good book," she said, catching the direction of my gaze. "You can borrow it if you want. I've already read it several times."

"I'm not much of a book person, especially after today. I was stuck in the Academy's super-secret library the whole day, reading stuff that made no sense."

"A library? I haven't been to a library in years."

The wistful way she said it gave me pause.

"Why years?"

She shot me an odd look. "Once a human says yes to Uttira, they don't leave."

"Trammer left all the time."

She looked away, swallowed hard, and nodded.

"He did. Only him, though, because of a spell that prevented him from saying anything once he left the barrier."

"So you're stuck here like me?"

She met my gaze again, frowning this time.

"Not like you. You can go wherever you want in Uttira. Attend school, make friends. Definitely not like you."

"Wait. You don't have to go to the Academy?"

"Have to? I'm not allowed to go to the Academy. I'm enrolled but complete all my work online. The groceries are delivered. With the exception of my other duties, I'm not supposed to leave the house."

My envy over her not needing to attend school disappeared as I understood what she was telling me. She was a prisoner in this house, locked in with her grief and as desperate to escape her confines as I was mine. Only, she'd chosen this.

"Why are you staying here then?" I asked.

"Because this is the only world I know. And, if I leave, I'll know nothing. Maybe not even my name. Adira explained how the spell works. It takes days from you. Years. It doesn't select which memories. It takes all of them. I've been here since I was a toddler. I'd lose who I am."

"Why can't they just put a spell on you so you can't say anything?"

"A binding spell? I'd accept it if that were an option. But, the Council ruled that no underage human shall be bound to Uttira. It prevents human parents from binding their kids without giving them a choice."

"When do you turn eighteen?"

"Another year and a half to go," she said. Her eyes welled up, and she blinked a few times. "I wish my uncle wouldn't have died."

I couldn't say the same. Her uncle had done bad things and had sounded like he would have done more if given the chance. But, I did feel remorse at my part in his death because of how hurt Ashlyn was now.

"I know what it's like being stuck where you don't want to be. Do you want to come to my place? We can see if Eliana wants to watch a movie and have a girl's night."

Ashlyn was already shaking her head.

"I like Eliana. She's nice. But it's dangerous for me to leave the house. It's warded for my protection. I can't get hurt here."

The injustice of Ashlyn's situation poked at my temper and showed through in my tone when I spoke.

"Yet, the Council makes you sit in the Roost."

"It's warded, too."

"Okay, this is ridiculous," I said, standing. "I get why you're staying, but you're living like you're in prison with work release duties."

"What other choice do I have?" She sounded tired. Beaten.

"I don't know, but I'm going to find out. Do you have something I can write on? I want to give you my number. If you need anything, call me. And, that's not an empty offer. Call me."

She got up and found me a piece of paper and a pen, and I quickly wrote down my number.

"I'll be in touch soon, Ashlyn." I reached out and gently gripped her arm.

She set her hand over mine.

"My uncle told me you were raised in the human world. Thank you for not being one of them. For being different."

I wasn't sure how to respond to that, so I gave her a pathetic excuse for a smile then left. No matter how much I wanted to deny it, I was a creature of the gods. Yet, I hated the rules that came with what I was.

I PARKED in front of the Quills' and shoved my way out of the car. My anger had only built on the drive over. Not dangerously, but close. I didn't understand why, exactly, when there wasn't anyone even around me.

Pounding on the front door, I waited. Mrs. Quill didn't leave me standing outside for long.

"I need to speak to you, Mr. Quill, and Adira," I said.

"Come in. You look upset."

"I am," I said, stepping into the entry. She immediately led me to Mr. Quill's study where he sat at the desk.

He looked up as we entered.

"Megan would like to speak with us and Adira."

He stood and pulled his phone from his pocket. A quick call later and a portal appeared. Adira stepped out and gave me a kind smile. For some reason, that tweaked my anger further.

"There's nothing to smile about," I said. "I just came from Ashlyn's house. Some creatures are meant to be solitary. Not humans. Not Ashlyn. The situation you've created for her is cruel."

Adira frowned. "Cruel?"

"The rules of this place mean she's pretty much under house arrest. She's grieving and utterly alone."

"That's why we sent you to visit her."

"I'm not enough. If you value the humans who are here, then start treating them better. Definitely not like prisoners in their own homes. You say you're teaching the students of Girderon Academy to blend with humans, but you're not. You're teaching them to keep apart from humans with your segregation that forces the humans to remain in their special little locations. And, by doing that, you're also teaching your youths that humans have a certain place in life. That they are lesser than us. Trammer's crimes don't solely lay on his shoulders. He is a product of the treatment he and his family received here. If you don't want something like that to reoccur in the future, things need to change."

I felt a tiny bit better that they'd listened during my entire rant instead of trying to interrupt or defend their actions.

"What do you propose?" Adira asked.

"If you want to really teach about blending, give Ashlyn the choice to attend the Academy if she wants. You said no one can get hurt within those halls. And, she's starved for contact with people her own age."

"The contact may not be what she anticipates. Many of the students still do not have control over their instincts."

"Well, they're there to learn, right? And, when the students see the staff treat her with respect and kindness, they will be more likely to follow suit, not just here, but in the real world too."

"Is there anything else?" Adira asked.

"Yeah, this town should have a library. It's big enough by human standards."

"We have no use for a library," Mr. Quill said.

I struggled to control my annoyance.

"You're missing the point. The whole goal is to train the next generation how to blend, right? A library is normal. Most towns have them. Normal humans go to them all the time."

"You've been to a library?" Mrs. Quill asked.

"It's been pointed out to me that I'm not human or normal, but yes. I have been to a library." I looked at them, my frustration growing because they weren't understanding what they were doing to the humans in Uttira.

"Did any of you have pets while growing up?" I asked.

Adira and Mrs. Quill nodded.

"We had a fish," Adira said.

I blinked in understanding. Sisters? Wow.

"Okay. Tell me about your setup for the fish. Where did it live?"

"We had a beautiful pond, shaded on one side by trees and open to the lights of the sun and dual moons on the other. It was a tranquil place. Our fish loved it there."

"Of course it did. It had space to move and grow. Freedom enough to be happy. Uttira is that pond for the underage creatures here. Except for the humans. The humans are in a glass bowl with only an inch of water. Just enough to breathe. Not enough to move. Just enough to not die. Do you get it? You need to make Uttira a tranquil, beautiful place for all the creatures here."

Mr. Quill nodded slowly while Adira and Mrs. Quill looked truly upset.

"You've given us much to think about," he said, standing. "Oanen, would you see Megan out so we can discuss this further?"

Hearing Oanen's name made my pulse jump, and I looked over my shoulder toward the door where both he and Eliana stood. I wondered how long they'd been listening.

"Yes, Father." Oanen's gaze shifted to me, and he held out his hand, a silent invitation to leave the room.

"Since you've always wanted to know how people make me feel in the past, I'm telling you now that you're all frustrating me. A lot. And I think if you continue to mistreat the humans here, after having been told that there is mistreatment happening, it's going to piss me off."

Adira nodded, a regal acknowledgement.

"We understand, Fury."

I nodded and turned to leave the room before pausing once more.

"And, that wasn't a threat," I said, looking back.

Mrs. Quill smiled. "Furies never threaten, Megan. They act. That's why we asked you to help Uttira. You've warned us and we, too, will act."

I nodded then continued to leave. When I reached Oanen, I glanced at the hand he still held out, and my pulse sped up. The thought of holding his hand heated my middle. Heck, the thought of touching him in any way sent jolts of naughty and nice through me.

"Come on," Eliana said, grabbing my arm and tugging me from the study. She led us down the hall to the living room she shared with Oanen.

"I hope they let Ashlyn attend the Academy," Eliana said the moment we entered.

"Me too. She's so lonely."

She nodded and sat on the couch.

"Are you staying for dinner?" she asked.

"Eliana, could you give us a minute alone?" Oanen asked.

Her eyes got wide, and she quickly hurried from the room.

"That was weird," I said, turning toward him.

"Not really. Instead of dinner here, let's go somewhere."

My stomach gave an excited flip then began to warm.

"Like a date?" I asked.

"Exactly like a date." I could hear the amusement in his voice.

"Okay." I could barely hear myself over the pounding of my heart.

He smiled slightly then reached for my hand. Warmth exploded inside me at the touch of his fingers against mine.

"You make it difficult to remember my promise when you look at me like that," he said.

"Like what?"

My breath caught when he leaned toward me. I knew what was coming. A kiss. And the thought jacked up the temperature already boiling me from the inside.

He stopped coming closer and just stared into my eyes, the heated look on his face blending with one of awe.

"You are so beautiful when your eyes glow."

He started closing the distance, and the thought of his lips touching mine delayed my reaction to his words. At the last second, I jerked back.

"What?" I said. Without waiting for an answer, I ran to the mirror above the sink in their kitchenette. I stared at myself then looked at him.

"My eyes aren't glowing," I said, seeing the normal brown.

"Not anymore. They were just a second ago. They stopped when you moved."

Panic settled in. Glowing eyes? Adira had mentioned a true form. Was I going through some kind of change? Right now? In front of Oanen?

I swallowed hard.

"I think I'll need to take a raincheck on dinner."

I raced out the door.

CHAPTER THREE

A GOOD NIGHT'S SLEEP AND NO REAPPEARANCE OF GLOWING eyes (or anything else even weirder) had muted some of my panic. But I couldn't let go of the incident. I kept envisioning Adira in her office, one moment human and the next, not. I needed to figure out what Oanen had seen and if it was an omen of something more to come.

After a quick text to Eliana to let her know I didn't need a ride, I drove to the Academy early, determined to scour the library for any reference to furies. Knowing what I was and the purpose behind my existence barely skimmed the surface of the questions I had. There had to be something more about furies. Which of the gods created us, and why had that god thought creating a female with severe anger issues a good idea? What the hell was up with glowing eyes? What else would happen to me?

Adira's comment about me having a true form kept coming back to haunt me. Why did the gods give us two forms? What kind of monster was I really?

Before I knew it, I was driving through Girderon's

main gate. Only a few cars sat in the parking lot when I came to a stop, and I walked the quiet halls without interruption.

The library door swung open at my touch. Setting my phone in the basket outside the door, I stepped inside, determined not to leave until I had some answers.

My eagerness faded as I skimmed through book after book. There was plenty of information on other obscure creatures I'd never even heard of. Draugr. Scylla. Níöhöggr. Echidna. Fylgja. Cave dwelling creatures. Snake women. Shapeshifting giants. Yet, nothing on furies except a vague reference in a slim book outlining the beginning of a war between the gods.

I read the meager three pages twice, trying to make sense of the story. But, it wasn't just the reference to furies that was vague. The whole book read that way. Some argument or event had happened that brought even more unrest and conflict to the already discordant gods. The resulting war consumed not only the realms of those squabbling immortals, but also the realm of man. Deaths noted "too numerous to endure" flooded the underworld with souls so greatly that even the furies stopped punishing the living wicked in their need to deliver souls to their master. It didn't say how the war ended, who won, or anything further about the gods or master of the furies. It only described the destroyed world of man, the much beloved mortal world all the gods coveted.

My stomach began to growl loudly long before a knock sounded at the door. I released the book I currently skimmed and let it fly back to its shelf as I stood. This time when I opened the door, Oanen stood against the opposite wall of the hall, his ankles crossed as he leaned in a relaxed pose.

"Expecting to wait a while?" I asked.

"Since that was the third knock, yes."

"Really? Sorry. I didn't think I was that deep into what I was reading. Not when it completely didn't make any sense."

He stayed in his relaxed position and lifted a hand, offering me my phone. Curious why he had it, I stepped closer. It wasn't until he hooked his arms around me that I understood he'd used it as bait. Before I could protest, he tugged me close.

I tripped forward, colliding with his chest, and he grinned down at me. One arm weighing against my waist, he lifted a hand and brushed the backs of his fingers along my jaw.

"Have dinner with me tonight, Megan."

I stared up at him with wide eyes as I struggled to breathe normally and swallow past the sudden dryness in my throat.

"Why are you so afraid of a simple dinner?" His soft question sent a shiver of hunger through me. The way he'd said it, I knew that dinner with Oanen wouldn't be simple. It would be full of his heated looks and my increasingly harder to deny need to touch him. A date with Oanen would likely end with a lot more than the touching we were doing now.

My gaze dipped to his mouth as I imagined just how we would end our night.

"Megan, I will break every promise I made to behave if you give in to what you're thinking right now."

I lifted my gaze to his and braced my hands on his shoulders. He started closing the distance.

"You are so incredibly warm," he said.

His exhale tickled my lips.

"Megan. Oanen. May I interrupt for a moment?" Adira asked, her voice coming from right behind us.

I jumped and jerked back. Oanen sighed and released me. Turning with an embarrassed flush, I faced Adira. The woman smiled kindly and addressed Oanen.

"I apologize for the intrusion. I heard you ask about dinner and was wondering if you could postpone it. There are a few liaison duties that require Megan's attention tonight."

She focused on me.

"We would like you to meet us at the Quills' residence after you're finished here. There are a few human recruits we want you to meet."

Any remnants of the good feelings I had from touching Oanen fled in a hurry.

"You're bringing more humans to Uttira after the talk we had?"

"Yes. But, it is because of your talk. As you said, humans are not solitary creatures. We believe that bringing more here not only replaces those we've lost but will help the ones who remain. I will see you after sessions."

Before I could open my mouth to argue further, she disappeared. Just vanished.

"Argh! I want to hit her," I said, looking up at Oanen. "All of them. They didn't hear a single thing I said. Bringing more humans won't fix anything for the humans already here. Why can't they see that?"

He reached for my hand, threading his fingers through mine.

"They will see. You'll make sure of that. Come on. Let's get you something to eat before your stomach gets any louder."

He began to lead me down the hall. I gently tugged my hand from his before my heart exploded, then wrinkled my nose as I realized I'd forgotten to eat breakfast and hadn't brought a lunch.

"I'll need to get a tray today," I said.

"Why? I packed you a lunch," he said, not commenting on my withdrawal.

"Thank you. You really didn't need to do that though."

He looked at me. "Did you enjoy yesterday's lunch?"

"Yes. It tasted better than anything I could make for myself."

"Then I'll keep making them."

The butterflies those words sent flying in my stomach had nothing to do with hunger.

We joined Eliana on the lawn outside. I sat beside Eliana, and Oanen sat on the opposite side of me, his thigh touching mine. Doing my best to ignore the contact, I handed him his lunch bag and opened the one he'd made for me.

"I can't find anything useful in that library," I said a moment before taking my first bite.

"I'm not surprised," Eliana said. "I mean, if you think about it, our kind was created before the written word was hugely popular. Most of our history would have been passed down verbally through the years. The stuff that's in there is likely from modern times when knowing how to read and write became more commonplace."

"Then why am I wasting my time in there?"

"Because some information is better than no information," Eliana said. "Adira doesn't do things that are a waste of time. If she wanted you to read the books, there's a reason."

"I wish she'd just tell me what that reason is."

"That's not how she works," Oanen said. "She's all about self-discovery and the importance of the struggle to gain knowledge. She says it gives the knowledge more meaning."

I sighed and kept eating my sandwich. How could struggling to learn the truth give the truth any more meaning than it had? It made no sense to me. However, as much as the library frustrated me, it was better than spending the day stuck in a classroom with other students.

THE QUILLS WERE WAITING for me at the door as soon as I came to a stop. Overhead, a familiar griffin soared, gliding on the currents and disappearing behind the large stone home. Oanen had followed me from the Academy. Likely, Eliana wasn't far behind. Although I wouldn't mind waiting for her, I knew that if I didn't hurry, I'd likely encounter a shirtless Oanen somewhere on the second floor. That motivated me to move. However, I wasn't sure if it was to meet up with him or avoid him.

The cold October wind whipped my hair around my

head the moment I got out of the car and rushed for the house.

Mrs. Quill smiled as I approached, and she offered me something to drink while Mr. Quill shut the door behind me.

"We have cider we could warm," she said.

"I'm fine. Thank you, though."

She nodded and led the way to the study. I didn't catch any hint of Oanen prowling the hallways, and any chance of interruption or eavesdropping ended the minute Mr. Quill closed the study doors behind us.

"Adira will be here in a few minutes," he said. "We should have a seat."

I took the chair facing the sofa. It gave me a good view of the room so I'd know the moment Adira did her magic appearance portal. The shimmer appeared only moments after I took a seat.

Adira stepped through first, followed by a boy around my age. I tried to hold back my initial surge of anger and took a moment to study him. Adira directed him to sit on the couch across from me and moved to stand behind him as he hesitated. I paid her little attention while I continued my scrutiny.

His dark hair fell in disarray around his head as his equally dark eyes flitted around the room, landing briefly on each of us. He looked unwashed and angry.

"Have a seat Michael," Adira said.

The boy sat with a look of belligerence in his eyes.

"I don't know what the hell is going on, but I want my fifty bucks," he said.

"Nothing bad is going to happen to you here," Mrs. Quill said. "We just wanted to introduce you to Megan."

All three adults looked at me. I didn't take my eyes off the boy.

"Hello, Michael," I said.

He stared at me without any hint of fear, and I didn't like that. Not one bit.

"Megan, we were considering inviting Michael to live in Uttira," Adira said, "and we would like your opinion."

"Don't you think you should be asking me my opinion on that?" Michael asked. "I like living where I'm at."

I continued to gaze at the boy, my anger rising. Why?

"Where do you live, Michael?" I asked.

"Depends on the night. I live wherever I want."

"Where do you live, Michael?" I asked again. My voice had changed though. I could hear the anger in it this time.

"New York. What's it to you?"

"I found him alone, living on the streets," Adira said softly.

Homeless. That fact didn't change the anger I felt toward him. Fury anger.

"What did you do, Michael?" I asked, leaning forward, wishing the coffee table weren't separating us.

"I don't know what you're talking about," he said.

"You've done something. Something not good. Tell me what you've done." I waited, focused on him, wanting to know his crime. I could feel it in my blood. In my bones. The anger...the rage...boiling hotter with each passing second.

"Tell me," I said again. "Confess your crimes." The words felt so right on my lips. And the need to scream them at him rose, nearly choking me. I struggled to control the urge.

"Confess," I said angrily. "Tell me what you've done."

Michael leaned forward suddenly, his eyes blazing with hate.

"I don't know what level of crazy you are, bitch; but you need to get out of my face."

I opened my mouth, ready to give into the urge, when Adira reached forward and set a hand on his shoulder, making them both disappear. The anger immediately vanished, but annoyance reared its head.

"That's who you want to bring here to keep Ashlyn company? That guy was—"

"Completely unsuitable," Mr. Quill said. "I hope you'll find the next one a better fit."

"The next one?"

"Yes, we have several candidates."

He'd barely finished speaking when the shimmer reappeared in the center of the room. This time Adira had two girls with her.

"Megan, this is Kelsey and Zoe. Sisters from Chicago."

The girls looked a little younger, maybe fourteen and fifteen years old. It wasn't their fearful expressions or ragged appearances that made my eyes water. It was the overwhelming odor.

"Hi," I said. "Not to be rude, but what is that smell?"

"Sewer," the older one said.

"Both you guys need a shower. The clothes need to be burned." I looked at the Quills. "I don't like what you're doing. Of course they'll say yes to whatever you offer them if you're pulling them from the sewers."

"No," one of the girls said. "We won't say yes to anything." She looked at Adira. "You said fifty dollars each to face a lie detector about how we ended up on the streets. We thought you were some kind of doctor. What was that glowing thing? Where are we?"

"You're in Uttira, a small town in northern Maine," Adira said. "The glowing thing was a portal. If you'd like to hear more, you're welcome to sit, and I'll answer whatever questions you have. If you'd rather leave, you only need to say so. I'll return you to your home and compensate you as promised."

The older sister glanced at the younger one.

"Let's just take the money, Kells. I don't like this place," the younger sister said.

"Most days, I don't either," I agreed.

Kelsey looked at me, frowning slightly.

"You might not like it, but you don't smell like someone else's crap, and you're not wearing the same clothes from a week ago." She turned to Adira. "We won't sit, but we'll listen."

"Uttira is a town for creatures created by gods long ago forgotten."

Zoe made a sound and said, "I told you," under her breath. I caught the word crazy too.

"It's easier to provide proof than to try to explain. Have you ever heard of a griffin?" Adira asked.

The doors to the study opened just then and Oanen strode in. His gaze met mine briefly then went to the two girls.

"Thank you for joining us, Oanen," his mother said.

He nodded and reached up for his shirt.

My chest cramped painfully as I understood that my newly acquired boyfriend planned to strip in front of these two girls.

"Since I already know griffins are real, I'll be going," I said.

I stood swiftly and started for the door.

"This is Oanen," Adira said, ignoring my exit. "He's a young griffin. He can choose to look like a human or—"

Just as I reached him, Oanen shifted with his pants still on, cutting off Adira's explanation. The metal button from his fly pinged off the wall by the door. Both girls screamed. The griffin paid them little attention. He moved quickly, stepping in front of me and blocking my exit.

I skidded to a halt, and he lifted his head. The feathers of his cheek brushed mine as he worried the hair by my right ear. Exhaling loudly, I reached up and smoothed my hand along his neck.

"You're lucky you sacrificed the pants," I whispered.

He clacked his beak twice then turned and left the room without shifting again. Realizing the girls had grown completely quiet, I faced the others. The girls gripped each other, their fear already having robbed them of color and voice. Adira and the Quills watched me with indecipherable expressions. Had Oanen told them we were together now? Or at least trying to be together?

Unsure and uncomfortable, I focused on the girls.

"It's real," I said. "The myths and legends we've heard are based on some very old truths. Werewolves exist. Griffins exist. Furies exist. That doesn't change the world you know, just your understanding of it. And you are as safe now as you were before you came here. Do you understand? Nothing's changed but your knowledge of the truth."

Kelsey nodded jerkily.

Mrs. Quill took over speaking.

"Adira brought you here to offer you a new opportunity. A new life. You could live here in Uttira. You would have your own home. All your bills would be paid. You would receive a human education and would want for nothing. In return, we ask that you help us teach the young of Uttira what it means to be human."

Kelsey met my gaze.

"What's the catch?" Her voice shook still.

"The catch is that you can't leave. Ever."

"Untrue," Adira said. "You can leave at any time. But we would remove any memory of your time here as a precaution to keep us, and you, safe."

"So we'd live here for the rest of our lives with everything paid for as long as we teach your young?" Kelsey hesitated over the last word, and her gaze flicked toward the door where Oanen had disappeared.

"Correct," Mrs. Quill said. "You would not teach all day, every day. While you're underage, you will focus on school and be asked to spend eight hours a week helping us. Your free time would be your own. Once you graduate, we would ask that you work forty hours a week, choosing from the jobs available in Uttira. You would receive pay in addition to the housing and support to which you will have grown accustomed."

I could see in their eyes that they would say yes. My stomach soured, and I felt like I'd just lost an important battle.

CHAPTER FOUR

THE NEXT MORNING, ELIANA'S CAR ALREADY SAT IN THE otherwise vacant parking lot. She leaned against her trunk, obviously waiting for me. I parked beside her and killed the engine.

"You shouldn't have taken off so fast last night," Eliana said as soon as I opened my car door.

"Eh, I'm pretty sure it was the safest choice for all of us."

I still felt pissy that the Council had trapped two more humans because of the desperation of their circumstances.

"Well, you missed the exciting news," Eliana said. "At dinner, Mr. and Mrs. Quill talked about Ashlyn and her need for more interaction. They've decided to let her attend the Academy if she wants. And not just Ashlyn. The new girls, too, once they're ready. And the Quills were asking me all sorts of questions about the things I remembered about the human world. I think they're considering building a library."

She grinned at me.

"Not bad liaising, Megan. You've started making some positive changes in just a few days."

"That's great." I returned her smile with one I didn't feel.

Although the changes truly sounded great, they didn't alter the way I felt about this place. Like a fish in a bowl with too little water, Uttira was beginning to feel suffocating. Maybe it wasn't Uttira but my own skin. After Oanen's spontaneous change from human to griffin last night, I couldn't stop wondering when that would happen to me.

"I need to get to the library," I said.

"Yeah. I know. Oanen's waiting for you inside. Maybe we can hang out soon?"

"Sure," I said, already moving toward the doors.

My rush wasn't to reach Oanen faster but to get to the books. However, the need for answers vanished when I turned the corner to the hall for the library. Oanen paced before the door. As soon as he heard me, he stopped. His gaze swept over me before settling on my face.

"Are you angry?" he asked as I approached.

"Want to hit something angry? No. Feeling a little frustrated? Yes." I stopped in front of him and tried not to notice the way the sleeves of his t-shirt hugged his biceps.

"I'm sorry about last night," he said.

His sincerity made me smile.

"What part exactly? Where you started stripping in front of two other girls or when you bit my hair?"

He cocked his head and considered me for a moment.

"You're not frustrated with me," he said with certainty and just a hint of relief.

"No. I'm not. I'm frustrated with this town and this stupid library filled with useless books."

He reached out and pulled me into his arms without warning. I melted into the embrace and let myself lean against his hard chest. I might have even closed my eyes and inhaled the scent of him. I couldn't be sure exactly because I was drowning in pure Oanen. The way we fit together. The way he held me, so tender yet so firm. It felt like I'd found where I belonged. Like I finally had a reason to be in Uttira.

His hands drifted over my back in a soothing, non-groping way.

"Don't let frustration get to you. You won't be stuck here forever."

He pulled back slightly, and I reluctantly released my hold on him.

"We'll get our marks soon enough and be able to go anywhere."

I nodded, not voicing my doubts. Would they let me leave if I no longer looked like me?

"I'll come get you at lunch. And we'll talk about our dinner date. Tonight. I'm not taking no for an answer."

I THREW the book in frustration. Before it could hit the wall, it changed course and slipped into its correct place on the shelf. I'd skimmed through over half the books in the library without seeing a single new reference to furies. There were more creatures than I thought possible. And if furies weren't mentioned in this collection, there was the very real possibility others weren't mentioned as well.

A knock sounded on the door. Ready to be finished with the day, I hurried to answer it.

"Any luck this afternoon?" Oanen asked.

During lunch, I'd vented about how my search for specific information was turning up nothing. Of course, I'd gone mute when trying to say what information. But, Oanen and Eliana had both encouraged me to keep trying before talk had turned to the impending date night and Eliana had fled.

"No. No luck." I stepped from the library and joined him in the hall. We started the walk to the parking lot exit.

"Don't give up. Talk to Adira. She might be able to point you in the right direction."

I rolled my eyes. To date, Adira hadn't been forthcoming with any information about me. Everything I'd learned, I'd learned on my own.

"Since you didn't say a time when you wanted dinner, I thought I'd come over at five," he said, changing the subject and creating a storm of nervousness that swirled in my stomach.

"Want me to bring anything?" he asked when I remained silent.

"No. I'll make everything."

Mostly just so I'd have less time to worry about what we'd do after dinner.

"Your heart's racing again," he said as he opened the door for me.

"Because the idea of having a dinner alone with you in my house is making me nervous," I said frankly.

"Would you rather go to a restaurant?"

"And risk someone ticking me off in the middle of our first date? No."

Oanen chuckled.

"I'll see you later then."

He didn't try to hug me goodbye, but he sure made it awkward by pulling off his shirt.

"I really don't like when you do that."

"I thought your issue was with someone else seeing." He handed me his shirt and cocked a brow, his hands hesitating at the fly of his jeans.

Many of the cars had already cleared the lot, including Eliana's.

"Just do whatever you're going to do, bird boy. I have a dinner to make." I turned around, ready to get in my car and leave. A pair of jeans hit me in my back.

I shook my head at the sound of his beating wings and turned around to pick up his discarded clothes.

"I changed my mind," I called. "You bring the dessert. And make it good since I keep having to pick up after you."

His eagle scream answered me as he climbed higher. Taking his clothes to the car, I sent a quick text to Eliana, promising to hang out with her Friday night, then started the trip home.

The internet and a stocked fridge kept me busy for the next two hours as I put together the mozzarella-stuffed chicken parmesan and a Caesar salad.

When I finished, I debated changing what I wore, which reminded me that I still had Oanen's clothes in the car. Playing it safe, I fetched his things and left them on the porch before settling in the living room to watch some TV.

I clicked through the channels absently, tension robbing me of the ability to focus. Nervous was a new thing for me, and I hated it. But, there was just something about Oanen. The more we spent time together, the more I was drawn to him.

The knock on the back door made my pulse jump. Wiping my hands on my jeans, I went to answer it.

Barefoot and holding a foil-wrapped pan, Oanen waited on the porch.

"Thanks for leaving out the clothes," he said, a slight grin tugging the corner of his mouth.

"Thanks for putting them on."

I stepped aside and let him in.

"It smells amazing in here. Lasagna?" he asked.

"No." I closed the door and followed him to the table, which I'd already set. "I figured you had that once already, so I went with something different. Stuffed chicken parmesan. What did you bring?"

He set the pan down and removed the foil.

"Eliana swore that you meant something chocolate when you said bring dessert."

I hungrily eyed the powdered brownies.

"Eliana is very wise," I said. "Ready to eat?"

"Sure."

We sat and started with the salad. My stomach wouldn't stop freaking out. Neither would my racing pulse. Although I knew he could hear it, he didn't comment.

"Eliana mentioned you two might be going to the Roost Friday," he said after I served him some salad.

When I'd texted her, I'd said to let me know where and

when she wanted to hang out. I'd rather hoped she would pick a movie night at my house.

"I guess. She wanted to hang out."

"You don't seem too enthused."

I sighed and played with my salad.

"It's not that. I do want to hang out with her. I'm just feeling off."

"Sick?"

"I've never been sick in my life."

"Me either. Just checking, though. So what is it?"

"I don't know. I'm just feeling..." I closed my eyes and tried to release the tension that had crept into my shoulders.

His hand closed over mine, trapping my idly moving fork. I opened my eyes and met his gaze.

"You can talk to me," he said. "About anything."

"Okay," I said, knowing he meant it. I took a deep calming breath and spilled my biggest worry.

"Adira said that how I look now isn't my true form, and I'm freaking out about what I might turn into. I don't know what I'll look like. When I'll change. Nothing."

"That's what you've been looking for in the library?" His thumb smoothed over the back of my hand.

"Yes, which really ticks me off for so many different reasons. What's the point of a super-secret library that almost no one can use if it barely contains any information? And, if I don't exist there, what else is missing? It's like I'm watching every other episode of a crime series. How can I piece everything together and see the full picture if I don't have all the clues?"

"Remember when I said Adira is big on struggling for

knowledge? It's the same for self-discovery. You'll figure this out."

"Before or after I turn into some raving monster?"

He released my hand and sat back in his chair.

"Is that how you see my true form? As a monster?"

He didn't look or sound angry, but that didn't stop my guilt.

"No. I like your feathers and wings."

"And my beak?"

"It's growing on me," I said with a slight smile.

"Your true form won't be any more monstrous than mine. And, while it might be different and take some time for you to get used to, you'll accept it as part of who you are. So will I."

"You're so getting an extra brownie for that," I said, picking up my fork. "Have I been missing anything fun by hiding in the library?"

"Not really. We've moved on to practical demonstration for the second half of the semester. I've successfully mastered the art of ordering takeout food."

"I hope you understand how useless that is."

"Useless to you and me but there are some who do need the practice. Remember the troll, Epsid? He tried ordering bone dust as a pizza topping."

"Wow." I finished my salad and excused myself to remove the chicken parmesan from the oven.

"Why are the parents not teaching these skills to their children at a younger age? If they learn from really early on, this wouldn't be such a big deal now."

"Some kinds hide their young away from everyone until

they reach eleven or twelve. By then, certain concepts are already set."

"Like eating human bones."

"Yeah."

I served Oanen one of the stuffed breasts along with a bed of angel hair pasta then served myself.

"I can't wait to see what you make for our next date," he said, cutting into his portion.

"Oh, I'm not cooking for the next one. You are."

He looked up at me, a grin pulling his lips.

"That's a deal. What kind of foods do you like?"

"Anything really. I've never been very picky."

We continued discussing favorite foods, books, movies, colors, and any other bit of information he could pull from me, or I from him, as we finished dinner. The conversation didn't stop at the table. It flowed through the clean-up and into the living room. There, it died a sudden death when he sat on the couch and patted the spot beside him.

"Do you want to watch a movie?" I asked, nervous once more.

"Yes."

Since I already knew he liked fantasy and science fiction because it amused him how wrong the movie industry got things, I picked out something that sounded interesting.

"Are you going to stand the rest of the night?" he asked when I hesitated to set the remote down and join him.

"Maybe."

"Megan." He stood and held out his hand over the coffee table. I clasped it and let him reel me toward his side. Without letting go, he sat then tugged my fingers until I sat beside him. Like the hug in the hallway, it felt right to lean into his side.

I turned my head and looked up at him. Our faces were close. Deliciously close. My pulse hitched higher.

"What are you so nervous about?" he asked, studying me.

I swallowed hard and went for brutal honesty, as usual.

"Kissing you."

"Why?"

"I don't know."

"Then, I think maybe we should just get it out of the way."

He closed the distance between us and lightly pressed his lips to mine. A bolt of heat shot through me at first contact. I inhaled deeply through my nose and reached for his shoulders, desperate for an anchor. He opened his mouth and licked the seam of my lips. I answered his silent plea and let him in. My senses flooded with the taste and feel of him, and I groaned. He changed the angle of the kiss a moment before his arms slid around me, pulling me into his lap.

A desperation crawled into my blood. A burning need to consume. To take. To release the wild thing I'd felt for Oanen since the moment he'd squatted beside me on the road.

I broke the kiss with a gasp for air.

He leaned forward and rested his forehead just over my pounding heart. His ragged breathing blended with mine for several long moments.

"Still nervous?" he asked.

"No. Now, I'm terrified."

And I mostly meant it. That out of control feeling now lingered just beneath the surface. It felt like I'd unlocked something, and despite his reassurances during dinner, I didn't want to know what.

"Me too," he said softly. He lifted his head and met my gaze. "I'm terrified of losing you."

He tucked me more firmly against his chest then nodded toward the TV.

It took some effort to pull my gaze from his perfect face and watch the show, but I managed. His fingers wove slow circles over the skin of my arm, relaxing me enough that my heart began to settle into its normal rhythm.

ONE MOMENT I sat at the library table, frustrated with yet another book that told me nothing about what I would become; the next, I lay on the couch, pinned between Oanen and the back cushions.

A dream.

I snuggled into him, enjoying the cool feel of his chest against my hands. He made a sound in his sleep. Something between a moan and a groan. I slid my hand up over his shoulder, smoothing over the back of his neck, not stopping until my fingers touched his hair. Lifting my lips to his, I kissed him.

His tongue immediately danced with mine. Fire heated me, inside and out. This time, I let go of everything and lost myself to the feeling of being in Oanen's arms. Of his desperate kiss.

A sharp smell tickled my nose. Burned hair, like the day I'd tried to leave the barrier.

The remembered smell jerked me from my dream that wasn't a dream. I opened my eyes and saw we were on the couch, but it was daylight.

With a gasp, I pulled back from Oanen.

"Best way to wake up," he rumbled, a sleepy grin tugging his lips. He opened his eyes, and the hint of his grin faded.

"Your eyes are glowing again," he said softly.

I flew off the couch and ran for the bathroom. This time, I caught the glow before it faded. I clutched the sink, staring as the normal brown replaced the vibrant orange. Then I started to shake.

"Megan, it's okay," Oanen said from behind me. "Your eyes are amazing no matter what the color."

I faced him, my gaze falling on the scorch mark on his pale blue t-shirt. A handprint on his right shoulder.

"My eyes aren't the only thing changing, though, are they. Turn around and show me your back."

His expression, always so carefully guarded, changed ever so slightly. Worry.

"Megan, it's fine," he said.

My stomach cramped with fear and self-loathing.

"Turn around, Oanen, or leave."

He sighed and turned around. The skin on the back of his neck was red as if sun burned. That wasn't the worst of it. Some of his hair had melted all the way to his scalp. I could see the outline of three of my fingers.

"This can't be real," I said to myself. "This isn't happening."

He turned toward me.

"Megan, we all go through some awkward changes. This is no different. You'll be fine."

"Me? I could have hurt you."

"No. You can't. You'll see. By lunch, you won't even be able to tell anything happened."

My thoughts jumped, connecting what he said with what I needed to do. Lunch. The Academy. Talk to Adira.

"Yeah. Sure," I agreed, feeling sick. "You're right. It'll be fine. I need to—" I swallowed hard. "I need to get ready. I'll see you at school, okay?"

He stepped forward and pulled me into a hug, holding me tightly.

"I know you're panicking. I can hear it," he said against my temple.

"After what I just did, I'm allowed some panic time."

"Fine. But if you don't show up at the Academy, I will come, and I will find you. Because one little burn hasn't changed a thing. I still want you."

He pressed a kiss to my forehead then left.

CHAPTER FIVE

I STILL HADN'T STOPPED SHAKING BY THE TIME I PULLED INTO the Academy parking lot. What the hell had I done? Although the practical, human-centric part of my brain wanted to dwell on the fact that I'd kissed Oanen first thing in the morning without brushing my teeth, the bigger non-human issue won.

"I almost cooked my damn boyfriend," I said under my breath. Who did that? What the hell was wrong with me?

Weeks ago, my mom had come to this place and registered me as a student. I'd seen the file Adira had on me. "Fury. Fourth Generation," it had read. Although additional information had been almost non-existent, the note had been there. Made by Adira. Likely, the very person my mom had talked to. Maybe Adira knew more. But, would she be willing to share what she knew? Probably not. And that really pissed me off.

I got out of the car and slammed the door, the early morning noise startling the few birds still in the skeletal, late-fall trees. Their flight brought my attention to the roof.

Oanen stood at the edge, looking down at me. My pulse jumped at the sight of him.

Crap.

Another car pulled into the lot as we studied each other. I needed a way to distract him for a few minutes so he wouldn't try to meet up with me in the hall. I really wanted to talk to Adira alone.

"I forgot my lunch again," I called. "I hope you had time to pack me something good. And a brownie. I really could go for another one of those."

"Yeah," a guy said with a laugh. "Now we're talking."

I glanced back at the guy and girl crossing the parking lot.

"Heathen," the girl said, giving me, then him, a glare.

"What?" he said. "Brownie wings are considered a delicacy by just about everyone. It's not like the brownie dies. Why do you think so many of them don't have wings?"

The guy winked as he passed me. The girl stomped ahead. I stood there in complete horrified shock. I would never be able to eat the chocolate dessert again.

Recalling Oanen and my request for the brownie, I looked up; but he was gone. Hopefully, on his way to get me lunch instead of wandering the halls.

Impatient to find Adira before Oanen found me, I jogged into school and headed toward her office. Oanen didn't appear in the halls, and I reached Adira's door without problem. Pausing for a moment, I took a deep breath to shake off some of my agitation before knocking.

"Come in," she called.

I opened the door, relieved she was in early, and quickly took the seat across from her desk.

"Good morning, Megan," she said, closing the folder in front of her. "You look upset. Is everything all right?"

"No."

Now that I sat in front of her, I realized the stupidity of my action. Did I really want to admit I had a dream about making out with Oanen then woke up to find out I'd actually been making out with him and burned him in the process? No. I one hundred percent did not want to talk to her about that.

"What happened?" she asked when I remained quiet.

"I, uh, think I almost started a fire in my sleep."

She smiled her usual, kind smile.

"There is absolutely nothing to worry about. Your house has been warded against fire, the same as the Academy, Roost, and any other public place. That means the structure and everything within it will never suffer any damage from flames created normally or magically."

"Oh." Her calm answer confirmed two things. She did know what I'd become because she hadn't denied the possibility that I could start a fire. And, whatever I would become did indeed have the ability to burn things.

"You see?" she said. "You have nothing to worry about."

Oh, I had plenty to worry about. If the house and everything inside of it was protected, then how had I managed to burn Oanen? Instead of demanding answers that I knew she'd be unlikely to give, I struggled to find a hole in her logic.

"How can I cook then? I mean, the stove is technically damaging everything I cook, isn't it?"

"The flames aren't damaging the food. They heat the pan which cooks the food. A loophole."

Maybe Oanen was a loophole, too, somehow. I needed to know how to make him not a loophole.

A piece of what she'd said finally registered. Why ward all the public places against fire along with my home? And why point that out to me? Because whatever was happening was going to get worse?

"I'm worried I might accidently hurt someone because I have no idea what's happening to me. But you do. And I'm struggling not to be completely pissed off that you're not telling me what I need to know." I met her steady gaze. "Not just what I am now but what I'll become. My true form. And it must be pretty bad if you've warded most of the town against me."

She folded her hands on the desk and leaned toward me with worry in her gaze.

"Not against you. From accidental fire. Megan, right now, you're focusing on all the wrong things. You need to concentrate on what's important.

"Continue to study the information in the library and perform your tasks as temporary liaison, which does require your attention. Ashlyn is due to visit the lake later this evening. She needs you to accompany her. I suggest you spend your time focusing on water dwelling creatures rather than a fruitless search about your lineage's history."

"So there's nothing about furies in the Academy library?" I asked.

"No. Nothing useful. Shall I tell Ashlyn to expect you after the final bell?"

"Yeah. Sure," I said, standing and moving toward the door, seeking escape before I did something really stupid.

"Megan," she called before I could step out.

"Yeah?"

"Your hands are fisted. If you've sensed someone wicked, you need to tell me. We don't want any more incidents like Trammer."

"No. No one wicked," I said. Just a crap ton of people being narrow-minded and getting on my nerves.

I left her office and went straight to the library.

For the next three hours, I learned what I could about hippocamp, naiads, mermaids, sirens, and many other water dwelling creatures. The scant details on how to identify them, what they liked to eat, and their preferred habitats didn't amount to much. If it had all been in one book, it would have taken me thirty minutes to read.

By the time Oanen knocked, my frustration at the information in the library had pushed back thoughts of what had happened that morning. The way his intense gaze locked onto me the moment I opened the door, though, brought it all back. The skin along his neck didn't look red anymore, but he'd gotten his hair cut closer to his head, a sure sign the hair hadn't magically grown back. Guilt and fear kicked me in the gut. We were making a mistake pretending I could be what he wanted.

"Don't," he said, snagging the front of my shirt and tugging me the rest of the way from the room.

"Don't what?"

"Run and hide. That's not an option for either of us."

Maybe not for him, but it seemed like a decent option to me.

"Did you bring me lunch?" I asked, needing to change the subject.

"Of course."

We walked through the cafeteria and found two bags waiting in our normal spot.

"Brownies, as requested. The kind without wings," he said, handing me one of the lunch bags.

"Thanks. Where's Eliana?"

"Spending some time with Ashlyn, getting her ready to start attending school next week. Mom took them shopping outside Uttira. Eliana convinced Mom that humans skipped school all the time and a day away from Uttira would make Ashlyn feel better. How about you? Today going any better?"

The tension coiled inside me, along with the ever-present need to just hit something, made the answer pretty clear.

"Not really. Adira told me to quit trying to find anything about furies because it's not there. So I'm reading about—"

The stupid spell kicked in, and I lost my voice. Rolling my eyes, I took a bite of my sandwich.

Oanen chuckled and started eating, too.

My break from the infuriating monotony of the library ended too quickly. After Oanen walked me back, I struggled to focus on the words on the pages before me.

A restlessness crawled under my skin, much like it had back when I lived in the city with Mom, so I gave up and lifted my hand from the book. As it slid neatly back into place, I collected my phone on the way out. I didn't care that it was still the middle of the day.

I wanted to hurt something, and I didn't want that to

happen here, not with Oanen around. I sent him a quick text to let him know I was leaving early then drove home.

However, being home didn't help my mood. I stood in the kitchen for one undecided moment then left again, on foot. While running in the city hadn't been smart for me, running here posed much less of a problem. Especially with so many of my peers occupied at the Academy. So, I let loose and sprinted toward the barrier, the only other place I knew that wasn't in town.

I didn't stop running until the winding road straightened out, and I felt the tingle of magic on my skin and could smell the lingering odor of burnt hair. Not even winded, I turned around and headed back the way I'd come.

When I arrived home for the second time, I felt a little better and went for a shower.

ASHLYN WALKED out of her house as soon as I pulled up. She didn't smile or wave as she walked toward my car and got in. Her eyes looked slightly red like she'd been crying. After a day of shopping, I would have thought she'd feel a little better.

"Is everything okay?" I asked.

"Yeah." She buckled her seatbelt and faced straight ahead.

"Um…try again because I'm not buying that answer."

She turned to look at me, tears welling in her eyes.

"I had fun today shopping with Eliana and Mrs. Quill."

She said it like she was confessing to a crime. Since I

didn't want to punch her, I doubted any crimes were actually involved. So, I waited patiently for more information.

She sniffled and wiped at her eyes.

"My uncle just died, and I was eating at a mall and laughing. What kind of person am I?"

I considered her for a moment.

"A sane one," I said. "I don't know what death means for the people who are leaving us, but I know what it means for the people left behind. It means hurting. But, only at first. The pain starts to ease to let the memories in. The good ones. We're meant to remember. To smile and laugh. It honors the one who has left us.

"People aren't meant to live forever, Ashlyn. We will all die at some point. What we do in this life will influence how we're remembered by those we leave behind. We're supposed to keep living even as we say goodbye and remember those who have already departed. You did nothing wrong."

She nodded and wiped her eyes again. Seeing that she was pulling herself together, I eased from the curb.

"You've lost someone?" she asked.

I paused, wondering how I'd known to say what I'd said.

"No, I've never had anyone to lose," I said. "It must have been something I heard my mom say at some point."

But I knew it wasn't.

We drove in silence only interrupted by Ashlyn's quiet directions to whatever lake we were going to. The term "lake" did not correctly describe our destination. I saw it through the trees as I made the last turn. The enormous body of water shimmered in the evening sunlight.

The road ended with a gravel parking area, a portion of the space sloping directly into the lake's edge. A slim trail led to a pier that extended at least twenty feet into the water. A bench beckoned at the end of it.

"Wow. It's pretty out here," I said, pulling to a stop.

"Yeah. I guess."

Ashlyn got out and started walking. I followed, wondering at her tone.

At the end of the pier, a fishing pole and tackle box waited on the bench. She picked up the pole, added a fake lure, and gave an impressive cast. I wasn't sure what I'd expected her to do, but fishing hadn't even come close.

"I've never been fishing," I said, sitting on the bench. "Is it hard?"

"I don't think what I'm doing qualifies as fishing," Ashlyn said.

"What are you doing then?"

"Letting the lake people know I'm here, I guess."

I looked out over the still waters and thought of all the creatures likely in its depths.

"Why?"

"Some of them can't or won't come to the Roost for practice. So I come here. They learn how to avoid the hooks that fishermen cast out, and they attempt to lure me into the waters."

"How do they do that?"

"Sometimes they sing. Sometimes they try to trick me."

"Have they ever gotten you into the water?"

"If they had, I wouldn't be standing here. My uncle was good at keeping me safe."

A twinge of pity rose for Ashlyn. This was something the Council had forced her to do. Something she'd always done with her uncle. They hadn't even given her a week to grieve before sending her back out again. This time with me.

The restless feeling I'd thought I'd exercised away returned, and my mind raced to find a topic that would distract us both.

"What did you think of shopping with Eliana? Was she picking out crazy outfits for you to try on?"

Ashlyn snorted a laugh.

"Yep. It was pretty weird. She kept picking out little girl type clothes for herself but handing me clothes that would make a prostitute blush," she said.

I chuckled.

"She did the same to me. Did you find anything interesting?"

She glanced back at me with a smile.

"Lots of stuff. Wanna see a picture?"

With one hand, she held the pole. With the other, she reached for the phone in her pocket. The device caught on her shirt and tumbled from her fingers toward the water.

Time slowed as she grabbed for the falling phone.

I started to stand to tell her to leave it as a green-grey arm rose from the water. The webbed fingers clamped around Ashlyn's arm and tugged. Ashlyn, already leaning forward, lost her balance and crashed into the water with a splash.

Without a thought, I dove in after her.

In the murky depths of the lake, I saw Ashlyn's struggling form caught by a creature with a tail and a mass of green hair. I grabbed a fist full of the floating tendrils and pulled hard.

The creature screeched, the sound hurting my ears even under water. Releasing Ashlyn, it turned and swiped at me. Its nails raked over the skin covering my ribs, just below my left breast. Pain ignited, burning me from the inside.

As I choked on rage and water, an orange light grew before me, illuminating enough that I could vaguely see the shape of a face through the hair. I drew back my fist and hit hard, the water barely slowing me.

The creature's head snapped back. Her whipping tail stilled, and she slowly sank. Not taking a chance, I gave her face an extra kick.

Whirling toward the tug on my arm, I drew back, ready for more until I saw Ashlyn. As soon as I faced her, she started toward the surface. I followed, breaking through seconds after her.

"Get out, quick," I said, pushing her toward a ladder fixed to the end of the pier.

She scrambled up and flopped onto the deck, staring at the sky as she gasped, coughed, and sputtered.

"Are you all right?" I asked, kneeling beside her.

"Fine," she rasped. "Damn phone."

I stood.

"I want that phone found and returned now," I shouted at the lake.

A minute later the device came soaring out of the water, straight for my head. I caught it easily and glared at the placid surface. I wanted to jump back in and beat the shit out of anyone I could find.

"Does it still work?" Ashlyn asked, sounding a bit better.

I looked at the phone, saw the lit screen, and handed it to her.

Her expression grew a little wary as I held it out.

"What?"

She flinched a little at my tone. I hadn't been able to keep the anger out of it.

"I'm not mad at you," I said.

She nodded and tentatively accepted the phone.

"I figured. I've just never seen your eyes do that."

"Do what?"

"Glow with flames."

"That makes two of us. I think we're done here. I'll drive you home."

I helped her to her feet and, ignoring the pain in my ribs, returned her to town.

Once I was alone in the car, I lifted my shirt and looked at the three cuts marring my skin and oozing a dark green slime.

"Fucking mermaids."

CHAPTER SIX

LIGHTNING HIT ME REPEATEDLY, SCORCHING THE SKIN OF MY stomach and creating a funnel of agony that sank into my very bones. I lay on the ground, unable to move and struggling to breathe. The dark mists floating around me created a damp film on my skin, adding to my misery.

Another bolt hit. I opened my mouth and screamed long and loud, raging at the skies to leave me in peace. The sound of my ragged inhale changed my surroundings.

The mists dissolved, and I blinked up at my bedroom ceiling. Everything ached. Not just where the mermaid had scratched but all over. My sweat-soaked clothes clung to me as I untangled myself from the damp bedding and sat up.

The bedside clock showed that my alarm had gone off over an hour ago. I was late for school, not that I really cared.

With effort, I stood and thumped down the stairs, making my way to the bathroom. I'd expected my reflection to look like I felt. Instead, other than being sweaty, I appeared fine. I turned on the cold tap and took a long drink. It helped cool the heat that seemed to be burning me from the inside. It didn't help stop the sweating, though. Needing to cool off and get clean, I started the shower then stripped.

Before I stepped into the spray, I checked my scratches in the mirror.

The long oozing gashes from the day before were completely gone. I ran my hand over the perfect skin and wondered what it meant. I'd never healed like that in the past. The few bruises I'd managed to gain throughout the years had healed normally enough, as far as I could remember. I hadn't bruised often, though, and had never broken a bone or scraped my skin. I'd always thought I'd been naturally tough.

I took my time washing and even more getting dressed. When I finally picked up my phone, it was well into mid-morning. I had seven texts from Eliana, wondering where I was and worried because she'd heard about the mermaid attack. And, I had one from Oanen that was less than five minutes old.

It simply said, "I'll find you."

That message sent a shot of warmth through me. Unable to stop my grin, I went out the back door and stood in the center of the lawn, watching the sky.

Oanen didn't disappoint. As soon as I spotted him, he seemed to spot me. He folded his wings and dove sharply, opening them at the last minute and landing as he shifted. The impressive display of power made my heart pound. The sight of the bare expanse of his...everything, made my knees weak. I could barely keep myself from drooling as he stalked toward me.

"Are you all right?" he asked.

"I am now."

He pulled me into his arms and hugged me close. The brief press of his lips against my temple began to heat my insides, and I tried not to think about what he so easily did to me.

"If you wanted to skip out today, you should have told me. I would have kept you company," he said.

"It wasn't an intentional skip out. I promise. I overslept and was a little slow to get ready. I just saw all your texts now."

"I only sent one."

He released me, and I quickly stepped back, creating enough space so I'd keep my hands to myself.

"Yeah, well, Eliana sent seven." I grinned. "I think there's a spare set of clothes in the guest room if you want to stay for lunch."

After he dressed, we ate a quick lunch I'd made while waiting, then he rode with me back to the school.

"So do we all heal quickly?" I asked just before we reached town.

"Not necessarily. Often it depends on the type of injury."

I made a noncommittal noise. First my eyes. Now freakish healing?

"What does 'hmm' mean, Megan? Did something happen when you went in the lake?"

"Yeah. A fish with an attitude scratched me with her claws. It hurt like a bitch and was oozing dark green slime. And, this morning, the gashes are gone. All of them."

"Pull over." His words were more clipped and stern

than usual, and I spared him a quick glance. He looked pissed and barely in control.

"Please don't go griffin mode in the car," I said. "I really like being able to drive around."

I quickly slowed and parked on the shoulder. When I stopped, though, he didn't get out.

"Show me," he demanded.

"What?"

"Show me where you were scratched."

I couldn't stop the stupid grin that pulled at my lips as I tugged up my t-shirt.

"Did I really just pull over because you're worried about me?"

His gaze stayed locked on the unblemished skin of my stomach.

"Yes."

The clipped word made me grin bigger.

"I kinda like this."

He finally lifted his gaze to meet mine.

"I don't." He reached out and ran his fingers over my skin. My amusement fled, chased away by the heat of his touch and the intensity in his eyes.

"I don't like the position the Council has put you in."

"Your parents and Adira? It's no worse than the position they put Ashlyn in. What would have happened if I hadn't jumped in after her?"

"She'd probably be dead."

"Exactly." I tugged down my shirt, dislodging his touch. "I need you on my side in this, Oanen. Uttira's view of humans needs to change." I pulled back onto the road.

"I am on your side," Oanen said. "I'll always be on your side."

THE THREE TORTUROUSLY BORING hours in the library hadn't been enough to incite any level of excitement for meeting Eliana at the Roost. But, because I hadn't spent any real time with her all week, I forced myself into the dress she'd given me at school and brushed out my hair.

The dress seemed a step up from the last. The flowing skirt tastefully fell to just above the knee, and the modest neckline scooped to give just a hint of cleavage. The back packed all the wow. The see-through, stretch black lace panel of material started just below the neckline and ran to just above the swell of my butt. It was a dress that demanded no bra. I went with the flow and skipped the garment, knowing Eliana would be happy.

The drive to the Roost didn't take long. When I got out of the car, the music thumped as usual.

"This town needs some diversity in hang out spots," I mumbled, staring at the red doors.

I so did not want to go in. Based on the cars lining the street, the Roost was very busy. Busy meant more people. More people meant more of a chance that I'd flip my shit. And, odds were Oanen would show up at some point and probably witness me doing it, too. Seeing him get all upset and protective was cute. Seeing me bloody someone's face was not. Yet, despite openly acknowledging all of that, I reached out and opened the damn doors. I was obviously messed-up in the head.

Music blasted me as I stepped inside.

Tonight, the Roost seemed especially popular. Bodies clogged the dance area from tables to doors. It looked like the entire student body of Girderon had shown up. The bold ones were on the stage, publicly making out to the sultry voices of the sirens at the microphones.

"Perfect."

People bumped against me as I attempted to make my way around the crowded dance floor. The bumps I didn't mind. The grinds got old quickly.

Through the chaos, I spotted Fenris with his her-herd. His gaze met mine, and he grinned. I lifted a hand to wave in return, but my fingers never got higher than my head. Fenris' grin widened the moment someone's strong fingers wrapped around mine. Before I could elbow the person, an arm encircled my waist and anchored me to a familiarly hard chest.

I leaned my head back against Oanen's shoulder and looked up at his beautiful eyes.

His hold on my hand loosened and traced its way down my arm. I shivered at the sensation and closed my eyes. The room felt ten degrees warmer by the time he reached my ribs.

"Dance with me," he whispered in my ear.

I opened my eyes as he turned me in his arms and held me close. We swayed to the music, and I lost myself to the feel of him. The feel of his hands on my back. The feel of his shirt under my palms. The brush of his hips against mine.

Heat pooled inside of me, twisting and coiling. Oanen watched me closely as I stared at him.

Unable to resist any longer, I tipped my head up to him.

The barest hint of a smile touched his mouth before he lowered his head. His breath teased my lips while his fingers traced the lace where my bra should have been. Anticipation boiled me from the inside as he moved his hand upward to cradle the back of my head.

The first touch of his lips to mine made my breath catch. He tasted like hope and home. Like air and freedom. He tasted like he was mine, and I was his.

I gripped his shoulder, pressing against him so not a speck of space remained. He groaned and swept his tongue inside, taking and demanding and billowing the flames of need that roared inside of me even higher.

The faint scent of smoke touched my nose, and I broke the kiss.

"Not yet," he said before claiming my lips again.

The second kiss stole my will to think or worry. Oanen controlled me with each stroke of his tongue. Like a marionette, I responded to each pull of my strings and continue to sway against him.

When he grunted and finally pulled back, it took several blinks for reality to intrude. The sound of the music. The voices talking and laughing. The smell of something smoldering.

My gaze dropped to my hand where I still touched his shirt. When I lifted my palm, I saw the dark brown patch that outlined the shape of my hand.

Oanen gripped my chin and tilted my head up until I met his gaze.

"I'm fine," he said, his words almost nonexistent in the beat of the music.

"I'm not."

When I tried to pull out of his hold, he wouldn't let me escape. He wrapped his arms tightly around my waist and leaned in so his cheek rested against the side of my head. The position brought his lips close to my ear.

"You are fine," he said. "Just afraid. Don't be. Not when we're together."

That was exactly the root of my fears. Being together.

I reached up between us and pulled his shirt aside enough to look at the red hand print. This time, I'd blistered his skin right in the center of where my palm had rested. Being with him the way he wanted only seemed to cause him pain. We were both just kidding ourselves if either of us thought this would end in any way that didn't result in him lying on the floor, burnt to a crisp.

Tipping my head back, I looked up at him.

"I think this is a mistake."

His fingers pressed more firmly into my back.

"I know it's not."

I wanted to believe him. He seemed so confident, so sure that whatever was growing between us would work. I knew better. Life wouldn't give us what we wanted. Why should it? It hadn't ever cooperated yet.

"I appreciate your optimism, but I think we need to get real. I've burned you twice with just—"

Yelling and shouting broke out behind me. A tingle of annoyance raced up my spine, and I turned toward the back tables. An invisible string tugged me forward. I wedged my way through people, barely noticing when Oanen reached out to stop a few incubi from grabbing me as I passed.

Near the back, a group of bodies crowded around the

booth where Ashlyn usually sat. Worried, I pushed forward harder.

"Move, dammit!" I yelled at a huge boy. He turned back to glare at me but stopped short when he glanced over my shoulder.

"Hey, Oanen," he said, stepping aside.

Ignoring the boy and Oanen, I focused on the cause of the commotion. Two boys held Kelsey back from attacking another boy who was kissing the hell out of her younger sister, Zoe. Zoe's fingers clenched the boy's hair. At first, I thought her hold was out of passion, then I saw her tears and pale cheeks. Had Zoe looked like she was enjoying herself, I would have turned around. Seeing her being forced into a kiss, though, ignited my temper, not only at the boy but at the Council. Kelsey and Zoe had no business being "on duty" at the Roost already.

I rushed forward, grabbed the incubus's shoulder, and pulled him away from his prize.

He grinned at me.

"You'll get your turn after I'm done with these two," he said.

I hit him square in his still glistening lips. His head jerked to the side at the contact, and his eyes turned black. Zoe tried to step away, but his hold tightened on her arm.

"I'm not done with you, human. Not until I drink every bit of that passion you're trying so desperately to hide."

"Oh, you're done," I said.

He hissed at me and reached out to caress Zoe's breast. The girl whimpered at the contact, and I snapped.

"Touch her again, and tip the balance. Become wicked.

Become mine." My voice sounded strange to my own ears. Angry. Commanding.

The boy who gripped Zoe paled and released her. The ones holding Kelsey released her as well. Kelsey grabbed her sister and hugged her close. The pair shook together, their cheeks wet with tears.

"I'm not wicked," the incubus said, reclaiming my attention. "She agreed to kiss me."

"Asshole!" Kelsey yelled. "You tricked her."

"Darling, that's not my problem. She agreed. That's all that mattered."

"Are you sure?" I asked. "Because if that were true, I wouldn't be itching to punish you."

The boy narrowed his eyes.

"The fact that you haven't already, fury, means I'm right. I'm not wicked, and you have no fight with me."

"Maybe not as a fury, but as a pissed off girl, I sure do."

I laid into him, hitting his pretty face again and again. It took a lot more effort to make him bleed than it would have a human, but I didn't mind taking the time to do the job right. By the time I finished a few minutes later, he looked satisfactorily messed up.

"Next time, consider the consequence before messing with a human. There's always a bigger, badder monster out there; and that monster might take offense to what you do."

"The same applies to you, fury," the boy said, turning his head and spitting blood on the floor. When he looked at me again, there was retribution in his gaze. "There just might be more powerful creatures out there than you, who will take offense at what you just did."

"I look forward to hearing them complain." I turned my

back on the boy and looked at Kelsey and Zoe. "Can I give you two a ride home?"

"We have a car. We can't leave yet, though. Adira said until eight."

"And I'm saying now. If Adira has a problem with it, it'll be my fault, not yours."

Kelsey nodded and moved toward me, not releasing her hold on Zoe.

"We'll walk you out and follow you home," Oanen said from just behind me.

He led, and I followed the pair. No one messed with the girls, and everyone moved out of Oanen's way.

Outside, the cool night air brought my attention to my temperature. I hadn't realized how warm I'd grown inside.

"Thank you for your help, Megan," Kelsey said.

"Don't thank me. If I'd really been helpful, you wouldn't have been in there in the first place. You've only been in Uttira for a few days. Why did the Council have you working at the Roost already?"

"We wanted to know what we were getting into before too many days passed."

"You should have talked to Ashlyn, then. She would have been able to give you an honest view of life in Uttira for a human."

"Ashlyn? Is she human like us?"

I felt my temper twinge that the Council hadn't even introduced them.

"Human, and not a fan of this place. Hold on." I turned to Oanen. "Can I use your phone?"

"What happened to yours?" he asked as he handed it over.

"Where on this dress do you think I'd stash my phone? I left it in the car."

His gaze swept over my dress, and I knew he wasn't thinking of my phone. Trying to ignore him, I sent a quick text to Ashlyn to see if she was home and had time for some company.

Oanen's phone immediately rang. Eliana's number.

"Hey, we're almost there. What's up?" she asked.

I felt a twinge of guilt. I hadn't even thought of Eliana since arriving, and it definitely hadn't occurred to me that Ashlyn would come to the Roost willingly for a night out.

"The new girls had a run-in with an incubus. I was thinking they should have a frank talk with Ashlyn before attempting any more assignments from the Council."

Eliana was quiet for a moment.

"Are they okay?" she asked.

"Yeah. Just shaken up."

"We're pulling up now." The call disconnected, and I saw the blinker go on for the set of headlights coming down the road.

A moment later, Eliana parked and got out. She and Ashlyn both wore cute, modest dresses and sad expressions.

"Kelsey, Zoe, this is Ashlyn and Eliana."

"Hi, Ashlyn. Nice to see you again, Eliana," Kelsey said.

"What happened?" Ashlyn asked.

"Some guy tricked Zoe into making out with him in front of everyone. Then a few more guys came up and said they were next. I tried to stop them, but every time I looked one of them in the eyes, I forgot what I was doing. He wouldn't even stop when Zoe started to cry. He said the salt of her tears gave the kiss more flavor.

"Then Megan showed up, eyes glowing, and kicked his ass."

The asskickery hadn't been nearly enough now that I'd heard the whole story. I wanted to go back inside and find the guy again.

"Eyes glowing?" Eliana said looking at me.

"It's nothing." I definitely did not want to talk about my freakish changes just then. "Kelsey and Zoe were here because they wanted to know what it would be like for them if they decide to live in Uttira."

The door behind us opened and the incubus who'd met my fist walked out with his two friends. His eye had swollen shut and his bottom lip had puffed up on the right side. Despite that, he grinned when he saw Eliana.

"About time you acted like what you are. I warmed the little one up for you. You're welcome."

Before I could take a step, Oanen's hands settled on my shoulders.

"Leave now, Eras."

The boy's eyes settled on Oanen and his hold on me.

"Your parents' influence doesn't matter to me," he said. "I'm not going to cower and bow like the other mindless idiots inside. There's three of us, and that fury can't do a thing if we haven't broken any rules."

The door had opened during his little speech, and a familiar chuckle reached my ears.

"It doesn't look like your opinion stopped her from doing something to your face a few minutes ago."

The incubi parted, and Fenris strolled toward us.

"It's always fun when you show up, Megan," he said with a grin.

"Not sure I'd call tonight fun," I said.

He winked and looked back at the other guys.

"You're in no position to continue this fight. Go home. I'm sure your mother will give you some love after she sees your face."

Eras's face grew red, and his eyes blackened. I fisted my hands, more than ready for him to make his move. Instead of giving me another reason to hit him, he pivoted and stalked away, taking his little followers with him.

"You coming back inside?" Fenris asked.

"If Megan wants to go back in, that's fine. But, maybe we should postpone our night out," Ashlyn said, her gaze flicking between Zoe, Kelsey, and Eliana.

Eliana nodded, a look of guilt on her face.

"I think we'll all pass tonight," I said to Fenris.

He sighed and nodded.

"Next time." He turned and went back inside.

"I'm really sorry that guy kissed you, Zoe," Eliana said softly after the door closed.

I suddenly understood Eliana's guilt and shrugged out of Oanen's light hold to wrap her in a hug.

"You didn't do this; they did. And, you are not them," I whispered in her ear.

She nodded against me.

"Let's take this back to my house," Ashlyn said. "We can all watch a movie and talk Uttira."

I released Eliana.

"You're invited too, Megan. Oanen," Ashlyn said.

"Thanks, but I think it would be better for everyone if I

headed home. Take Eliana with you. If anyone can teach Kelsey and Zoe how to resist the creatures here, Eliana can."

Eliana tried to protest, but Ashlyn won her over quickly with a pleading look. The four of them walked away, leaving me alone with Oanen.

Sighing, I faced him. The fight had been a nice distraction, but it hadn't erased the issue of us. His shirt still hung open, and I could see the edge of the red handprint. I knew he wanted me to not worry about it. To go with the flow and pretend like it had never happened. But I couldn't. I'd hurt him just like I'd feared I would.

His gaze held mine, and he reached up to smooth back some of my hair.

"I know what you're thinking. You're wrong. This burn doesn't matter just like the one before didn't matter. Just like all the future burns won't matter."

Panic hit me hard right in the sternum. Future burns? Hell no!

He exhaled heavily.

"I'll let you run and hide for now, but only for a little while."

He leaned in and kissed me tenderly, creating a familiar heat in my middle. This time I had the sense to keep my hands to myself. Barely.

When he pulled away, I almost followed him.

"Don't make me wait too long," he said.

He touched me one last time then went inside.

CHAPTER SEVEN

AFTER TEN HOURS OF RESTLESS SLEEP, I ONCE AGAIN WOKE sweaty. Only this time, I was irritable, too. How many times did I need to hurt Oanen to prove to myself I wasn't good for him? I had no answer. Not even after breakfast or a long shower or a marathon of science fiction shows.

Frustrated, I wandered to the kitchen. A knock on the back door interrupted my mindless staring contest with the inside of the fridge. I looked up and saw a familiar face that lifted my mood a bit. At least, enough to answer the door without a scowl.

"Hey, Fenris. Sorry about last night."

"No need to apologize. I was just wondering if you might want some company today?"

I stepped aside to let him in.

"Running from your her-herd again?"

He grinned.

"So what have you been up to? Other than last night, I haven't seen you all week," I said.

"Nothing special. Sessions and pack stuff. Aubrey's actions led to a pack-wide inquisition."

"Spanish style?" I closed the door behind him and went back to the fridge.

"No. No jailing or torture, other than Aubrey."

"Yeah, what happened to her?"

"She was moved to another pack where she's being kept in isolation, only speaking with that pack leader. It's like a retraining program." He grew quiet behind me. "So what are you hoping to find in there?"

"Some miracle food that will solve all my problems. Know of any?"

He chuckled. "Nope. But, I hear talking about problems helps. I have good ears."

"And teeth and eyes, I bet."

"Only for girls who like to wear red."

I closed the fridge door and rolled my eyes at him.

"Seriously, tell me what's going on," he said kindly.

"I hate not knowing what I really am or what I'm capable of. Sure, I'm a fury. But, what the hell's a fury? My mom could have at least given me some kind of heads-up before she took off. If I'd known something, anything, about myself maybe I wouldn't be so freaked out."

"Why are you freaked out?"

"I've burned Oanen twice now without meaning to, and my eyes are starting to glow when I'm angry or...well, never mind. No matter what, burning people can't be good."

"Is Oanen mad that you burned him?"

I snorted.

"No. He keeps telling me it's no big deal. I don't know

what needs to happen for him to realize how dangerous I might be. Death by fire? He's insane for not seeing the risk."

Fenris studied me for a long moment before he wrapped me in a slow, comforting hug. I rested my head on his shoulder and released a long breath. I hadn't realized how much I'd needed a sympathetic hug until he gave it.

"Oanen's not insane," Fenris said quietly. "I don't think there's a guy alive who wouldn't suffer anything for the right girl."

"That's what I'm afraid of."

"I don't think you need to be. I'm touching you, and I'm just fine. You feel warm, but not hot enough to burn me. You'll learn control with Oanen, too."

I pulled back, and he released me, his gaze filled with compassion.

"Thank you."

"Any time. Now, how about we start making some dinner, and you tell me what else is bothering you?"

"Why do you think there's something else?"

"Because you said problems. Plural. So, spill it."

"You just want me to feed you."

He covered his heart with a hand and pretended to be wounded. Grinning, I opened the fridge again and pulled out what we'd need to make burgers.

"You're right. It's not just worrying about what might happen to Oanen. Uttira's getting to me. I can't stand the way the people here treat the humans."

I handed Fenris a tomato to slice and started forming patties.

"Maybe that's because you still see yourself as human," Fenris said.

"You're partly right. I know I'm different from them, but I don't feel like a completely different species. And I don't see how any other creature can view humans as so different when we all look like them. Why do we think our differences make us superior?"

"That's a good question."

I let the pan heat before putting two burgers in.

"See, that's what I'm talking about. There's no valid reason. The humans are treated the way they are because they've always been treated like that. You saw what happened to Zoe. If you had a younger sister, would you want some guy creeping on her?"

"No."

"Did you notice how I didn't say the species creeping on your pretend sister? You know why? Because I knew it wouldn't matter. No one wants to be treated like that."

"So what are you going to do about it?" he asked, taking two plates out of the cupboard.

"Uttira's attitude toward humans starts with the Council. Rules need to change in order to change perceptions."

"What rules?"

"The one where humans have to willingly be bait for all the creatures in Uttira. While I understand that the creatures here need to learn, it doesn't need to occur in a way that's threatening to the humans. Why not have them go to the Academy with the rest of us? They'd be in a more protected environment there. Ashlyn feels so segregated and fearful of her safety, she doesn't leave her house. And the Council encourages that behavior by having everything she needs delivered to her. Ashlyn should be able to run to the store if she wants, without worrying about someone trying to eat her."

I slid the two patties on the buns Fenris had waiting, and he carried the plates to the table. While we ate, I vented and he listened. He didn't agree or disagree with anything, just listened. When we finished, he helped me with the dishes.

"Thank you for listening," I said. "You're right. I do feel a little better."

He put the plate away and gave me his usual boyish grin.

"Any time. Just keep feeding me."

I hugged him, grateful to have a friend, and it made me realize just how much I missed having Eliana around. I needed to call her today and—

The door opened behind me. I pulled back from Fenris and turned to see who'd come in.

Oanen stood just inside the kitchen. Shock briefly showed on his face before all expression vanished. The only tell at what he felt was his hard, twitching jaw muscle.

Before I could say anything, he turned around and walked out. I ran after him, reaching the porch as wings started to unfurl from his back.

"Don't you dare take off without listening to an explanation," I said.

The wings folded and absorbed back into his skin. He didn't turn to face me, though. Instead, I stared at his amazingly naked backside.

"I think what I saw was explanation enough."

"What you saw was a hug between two friends."

The front door opened and closed. I knew Oanen heard

it, too, because he fisted his hands. I stepped off the porch, grateful that Fenris had left and given me the privacy I needed to talk to Oanen.

"Right. Friends."

"Friends, Oanen. Use your damn ears. Does Fenris make my heart race? Does he make me hot enough to burn him? No."

His hands remained fisted, fueling my already smoldering temper. I stalked forward until I stood just behind him.

"Given my disposition to most people, I know it's hard to believe that I might actually crave friendship. But I do. Finding someone who doesn't annoy the piss out of me is unbelievably rare. And, that's exactly why I need to keep the ones I have, no matter what the gender. Your jealousy isn't cute. It's infuriating. Either trust me or fly away."

He bowed his head for a moment then turned.

"Seeing you in someone else's arms hurt more than any burn you could ever give me."

"Because you're putting meaning into the gesture that just isn't there," I said. "I already feel so caged in this place. Don't cage me more because you're jealous."

"I can't change how I feel."

I briefly closed my eyes, struggling to control my temper.

"You can change it by trusting that what I feel for you I have never, and will never, feel for anyone else. You're choosing not to trust." I lifted my gaze to glare at him. The sight of his angry, red face pushed me too far.

When I opened my mouth, it wasn't my voice that echoed around us; it was my fury.

"Leave now, Oanen Allister Quill, before I pluck the wings from your back."

His wings erupted and wrapped around me at the same time as his arms.

"Take them," he said fiercely against my ear. "They're yours, like my heart."

His words penetrated the rage boiling in my mind.

"I'm sorry I doubted you, Megan. I won't make that mistake again."

I slowly exhaled in relief and hugged him in return. He winced slightly, and I immediately pulled back. It wasn't until that moment that I noticed the acrid smell of burnt feathers and scorched grass.

All the things I'd blocked out in my fit of temper hit me hard. I took a stumbling step back when I caught sight of his singed wings and the blisters on his chest and arms. His face wasn't angry red, just burnt red. Each retreating step crunched as I backed out of the blackened circle of grass around us. I'd done that. All of it.

"It's okay, Megan," he said, not trying to follow me. "I'm fine. Breathe. Just breathe."

I realized I was panting for air and stopped walking to brace my hands on my knees. I forced myself to take several slow, deep breaths. I started to shake. What the fuck was wrong with me? Who got that mad over a jealous boyfriend?

"I should have let you think that hug was something it wasn't," I said. "You would have been safe then."

A hand settled on my head.

"I'm glad you didn't."

I continued to just breathe as he ran his fingers over my hair. After a few minutes, the shaking stopped.

"I can't keep going like this," I said. "I need answers."

"Let me go inside and grab some pants, then we can go to my parents."

I nodded, not looking up.

A moment later, the porch door banged shut. I stood and stared at the damage I'd caused. Burned patches in the shape of footprints started near the back door and disappeared into the circle of blackened grass. The edges still smoldered, and wisps of smoke continued to rise up in the air. Inside the circle, twin patches of fall, brown-green grass in the shape of Oanen's feet remained untouched.

Turning away from the ravaged yard, I walked into the house. Water ran in the bathroom. While I waited for Oanen to reappear, I finished cleaning up the kitchen. By the time the bathroom door opened, I sat at the table.

When Oanen entered the kitchen, he wasn't wearing jeans but a pair of loose shorts I hadn't even known he'd left here. I understood the choice, though. All his exposed skin looked far too red. Some of it had blistered. Some of it had blackened and peeled.

I swallowed hard and averted my gaze, struggling with my guilt.

"All the burns in the world wouldn't come close to causing the pain I felt when I thought I'd lost you," he said.

I shook my head, unable to speak. He crossed the room and stood in front of me. Without a word, he held out his hand. I knew it was more than an offer to stand. He was asking for trust, just like I'd asked of him. I did trust him. But, could I trust myself? Both Oanen and Fenris thought I

83

should. Yet, the blistered palm held out to me begged otherwise.

I looked up at him.

"Why me?"

He studied me for a long moment, then his lips twitched slightly.

"Because you got my attention when no other girl could."

"I hit you in the face."

"You did. And after that, I couldn't look away. It's you, Megan. Always."

He crooked his fingers to draw my attention to the hand he still held out. Heart aching, I clasped his hand gently and stood. I stared up into his beautiful blue eyes and felt myself start to cry. Our fascination with each other was going to get him killed.

"Don't," he said, stepping into my space. He released my hand and cupped my face, his thumb brushing away the tear that spilled over.

His lips gently settled over mine, a light caress of shared anguish.

"We'll get through this. I promise," he whispered against my lips.

I nodded and stepped back, too afraid that I'd accidentally hurt him more.

"I'll drive you home," I said.

He followed me out of the house. Instead of letting him open my car door for me, I opened his and watched him closely as he eased himself inside. He masked his pain well, but I knew it was there in the way he didn't fully relax into the seat and the way his expression didn't change at all.

I tried to emulate him as I got in behind the wheel and kept all my worry from my face. When he reached over and put his hand on my leg, I knew I wasn't doing as good of a job at hiding what I felt as he was.

"What are your parents going to think?" I asked once we were on the road.

"Hopefully, that it's time to tell us whatever they know about furies."

Unwilling to steal his hope with my doubt, I said nothing; and the rest of the car ride progressed in silence.

Mr. and Mrs. Quill both waited by the door when I pulled up before their home. I parked the car and got out quickly, meaning to help Oanen, but he opened his door and stood before I could reach him. His mother's face paled at the sight of him, and her gaze immediately flicked to me. I could feel myself growing warm with my climbing anger. None of this would have happened if Adira would have just explained what I was.

Oanen reached out and threaded his fingers through mine. With a gentle tug, he led me to his parents.

"You have blood on your cheek. Are you all right, Megan?" Mrs. Quill asked.

I frowned and wiped at my cheek while wondering why she was asking about me and not Oanen.

"She's okay, Mom. She was crying," Oanen said.

"Blood tears? Already?" she said, sounding worried.

My gaze pinned hers.

"You knew I'd cry blood? What else do you know?"

She was already slowly shaking her head.

"Please," I begged. "Look at Oanen. I don't want to hurt him like that again."

Her compassionate gaze held mine for a moment before she waved us in.

"Let's talk inside," Mr. Quill said.

Oanen waited for me to go first then hung back to walk with his father, who I heard ask, "How bad are the wings?" Oanen didn't answer.

"Let's go to the study while Oanen cleans himself up," Mrs. Quill said.

No steps echoed ours on the stairs, and when I glanced back, there was no sign of Oanen or his father.

"Oanen will be just fine," Mrs. Quill said softly.

"This time, maybe," I said, continuing up the stairs. "But what about next time?"

"Are you so sure there will be a next time?" she asked.

"Since I have no clue what's happening, that means I have no control. No hope of stopping it. And, Oanen refuses to stay away. So, yeah, I'm pretty sure there will be a next time."

I walked into the study first but stopped short at the sight of Adira.

"You are only partially correct," she said. "You do know what's happening. You're coming into your fury powers. You cry blood, and you can generate enough heat to burn things or people. And you're unable to control it. Yet. However, your lack of control has nothing to do with your lack of knowledge about what you will become. You lack control because you aren't spending the time to learn who you are now."

I stared at her for two heartbeats. Annoyance crawled under my skin, but no rage. Not yet.

"You know, for a guidance counselor, you do very little

guiding. I don't need your bullshit answers right now. I need your help. And if you're not willing to give it, fine. Let me leave so I can find my mom. She owes me an explanation."

"I'm sorry, but that's just not possible. You cannot leave without your mark. And, you will not earn your mark until you learn to control your anger."

"You know what? This whole 'here to learn control and blend' thing is such a load of crap. I sure as hell do not feel like anyone is teaching me anything. All I see being taught is how to successfully hunt humans without getting caught. That's not control, and that's not blending. Take another look at your high and mighty Academy and see it for what it is. A training ground for the next generation of predators. You want peaceful coexistence? Start treating the humans like they have just as much right to exist as we do. And stop hiding the truth from everyone."

"What would you have us do?" Mrs. Quill asked.

"Start by giving me answers. Then, get rid of the humans' assigned duties. The duties degrade the humans in the Uttira residence's eyes. We need to stop thinking less of them, or you'll have another incident like Trammer on your hands."

"Without an opportunity to practice, how will our youth learn to control their urges?" Adira asked, completely ignoring my plea for information.

"Not my problem."

I turned to Oanen's mom. "Tell Oanen I'll call him later."

I took a step toward the door.

"You honestly feel you've learned no control since coming here?" Adira said.

"Yes. If I were in a crowded city, I'd be just as likely to punch someone in the face as I was before."

"Perhaps we should test that."

CHAPTER EIGHT

GOOD LUCK TONIGHT. CALL ME WHEN YOU'RE BACK.

I stared at Oanen's message for a second longer before turning off my phone and slipping on my jacket. Guilt continued to torment me. I needed to understand what was happening. The key to that was my mom. The key to reaching my mom was controlling my temper during an excursion with Adira. No problem. Right. I was so screwed.

Precisely on time, the shimmer of Adira's portal appeared off the back porch. I went outside just before she stepped through.

"Are you ready?" she asked.

"Yes."

"Let's see how well you can control your temper, then. Shall we?"

With the portal's shimmer still flickering behind her, she held out her hand. As soon as our fingers touched, my stomach twisted. The magic of the portal wrapped around us as she tugged me forward. One second, we stood in my backyard; the next, we stood on a city street.

I knew I was in trouble before I took my first breath. Waves of agitation crawled over my skin. Even though Adira and I stood alone, I could feel the people around us. Just the wicked ones. And these only felt mildly wicked.

"How do you feel, Megan?" Adira asked, watching me closely.

"Annoyed. What the hell happened to all the decent people in this world?"

Adira smiled slightly. "We happened. Many of the creatures made by the gods were created to corrupt the perfection of humanity."

"Bullshit. I'm not buying that. Why are the humans born all pure, but we aren't? Because that's what you're implying, right? That we are born to fulfill whatever purpose the gods set before us, but the humans get to frolic around like herds of goats, without any responsibility for their actions? No, Ashlyn has proven that humans have a choice. They can choose to ignore our corruptive influences."

"That would imply that we, too, can then choose to ignore our purpose and instincts."

Oh, she was good.

"I led myself right into that. Fine. I'll try to ignore mine."

"We shall see. Let's find the first candidate."

She started down the street at a brisk pace, and I hustled to keep up. She hadn't picked the nicest street. Dumpsters sat near the loading docks and back doors of businesses. The stink of rot overwhelmed the hint of fresh food being cooked somewhere else.

Movement by one of the dumpsters made me jump. Not

Adira, though. She walked right up to the huddled form in the shadows.

"Eugene, I'd like you to meet Megan. She's from my hometown." Adira stayed several feet back from the boy.

"Hi, Megan." The voice was young but weak. Almost listless.

I stepped past Adira, trying to get a closer look. The shape seemed small, balled up in a fetal position.

"Are you all right?" I asked.

"I'm trying to sleep on the ground near a dumpster leaking fluid that no sane person would want to be near. I'm great."

Something got under my skin, but it was light and easily ignored compared to the signals coming from the other people hidden further down the alley.

"You don't belong here," I said.

"If not here, where?" he answered.

"Where are your parents? Family?"

"Dunno. I left when they were high. When I went back the next morning, there was an eviction notice on the door, and my upstanding parents were gone."

"I'd like to offer you a real home, Eugene," Adira said from behind me. "A real bed. Three meals a day. A chance to attend school again."

The boy uncurled himself enough to look up at me and then Adira, his dark brown eyes now alive with interest. Underfed and dirty, but with a light dusting of dark hair on his chin, he looked about my age.

I hated this. What kind of choice was Adira really giving him?

"What's the catch?" Eugene asked.

"You lose the life you know, and you're trapped forever in a world you'll wish you never knew existed," I said before Adira could try to gloss over the reality of what would happen.

"So, you're telling me to pick between the red pill and the blue one?" He snorted and stood up. "The truth seemed to work out okay for Neo."

"Um, he died at the end of the third movie, didn't he?" I said, thinking he was missing the point.

Eugene shrugged.

"If I stay here, I won't have a long life anyway. Give me the reality pill, lady."

"Any objections?" Adira asked as she glanced my way.

I sighed. "There's nothing majorly wicked about him. At worst, he probably stole something to eat at some point."

"Two bucks from another alley rat's pocket," the boy said, unashamed. "He would have just traded up for booze anyway."

"Then it's settled," Adira said. "Come with us. You'll be showered and in a clean, warm bed within an hour."

Anger slammed into me like a baseball bat to the back of the head. I grunted and took a step forward from the force of it. Head hanging, I struggled to control the urge to fight. To punish whoever carried so much wickedness.

"Megan?" Adira said softly. "Are you in control?"

A scuff of movement from behind us announced the source of my affliction. I lifted my head, fighting a losing battle.

Eugene took a step back when my gaze met his.

"Holy shit," he breathed.

"This is the truth," I said, my voice echoing oddly.

"Watch. Then decide if a warm bed is worth the price of your ignorance."

"Eugene," a new voice said. "When did you start hanging with these high-class pieces of ass?"

The nails of my fingers bit into the skin of my palms as I clenched my fists tighter at the sound of the voice. I turned toward the newcomers. Three of them all dressed in dark clothing. Tattoos decorated the knuckles of one and the cheek of another. Their jewelry flashed in the distant dock light.

"Nice eyes," the first one said. "They contacts?"

"No." I walked toward them, my words coming from some hidden part of me. "Tell me your crimes. What sins will you confess?"

One of the guys burst out laughing. I hit him square in the mouth, the impact snapping his head back and sending blood flying onto one of his companions. He grunted and staggered. The friend with blood on his face pulled a gun from his pocket and aimed it at me.

"On your knees," I said, my voice scarier and more commanding than I'd ever heard it. Even as some part of me acknowledged something bad was happening, I couldn't stop it.

All three men fell to their knees.

"Confess."

That single word reduced the men to tears. They blubbered their way through stories of theft and attempted murder. The one with a broken nose barely made sense, but it didn't seem to matter. As they spoke, the need to make them pay for each crime increased until I felt bloated with it. I reached out and put my hand around

93

the first one's throat, lifting him off his knees. I felt no strain.

"Randall Aaron Walker, your wicked confessions have guaranteed your place in—"

"Megan, stop," Adira said.

Rage boiled inside me at being interrupted. She touched my shoulder, and my stomach twisted. My hand slipped from around the man's throat, and I landed on my back. I blinked up at the stars, confused and no longer fury angry, just angry.

Eugene's face appeared above me.

"What are you?" he asked.

"Pissed off," I said, getting to my feet.

Adira stood on the sidewalk, not far from me.

"Some kind of angel?" Eugene asked, still watching me.

The complete absurdity of his guess distracted me from Adira. I stared at the filthy boy in disbelief.

"What? No way. What kind of angel has fiery eyes?" I asked.

"The one who beats the crap out of the guys who've been dealing to my parents for the last four months."

"That life is done now," Adira said.

Ignoring me, she nodded toward the house attached to the front lawn on which I stood.

"Everything in this house now belongs to you, Eugene." She handed him a key. "Clean yourself up. Sleep. Megan will be here in the morning to pick you up for your first day at Girderon Academy."

"Not a chance in hell," I said.

First, I was still mad at her for talking this kid into coming. Second, I was still mad at her for stopping me midasskicking. Third, I would not let her continue to mistreat the humans in Uttira.

"You wanted the humans to attend the Academy."

"Yeah, but not on the first day here. You need to give Eugene time to understand what this place is. First, he meets Ashlyn. If he decides to stay, he then decides when he's ready to attend the Academy, or if he'd rather homeschool for a while."

"I really don't mind," Eugene said. "I like school. Saying it's an Academy makes it sound fancy. Fancy wouldn't be bad after the last few weeks I've had."

"I get it," I said, turning to him. "I really do. But you need to talk to Ashlyn first. I won't throw you to the wolves —literally—by sending you to Girderon without you understanding the most disturbing truth about this place."

"And what's that?" he asked.

"All those legends you thought weren't real? Well, they are. Werewolves. Mermaids. Giants. Magic. It's all here. And it's not rainbows and pixie dust. The Council brings humans here so those very same creatures of myth can learn to control their impulses."

"Impulses," he said slowly. "Like making bad guys confess? That doesn't sound so bad. Personally, I think you should do more of it."

"We're not all the same. Some have impulses to eat you."

He paled slightly, but I didn't regret telling him the truth. He needed to understand that he'd only traded the type of danger he was in; he hadn't left it behind. And, I thought he was beginning to get it based on the way he looked down at the key in his palm.

"Yeah. If you think talking to this Ashlyn is a good idea, I'm okay with that," he said after a moment.

"All right. I'll ask her to come over tomorrow night. It'll give you some time to settle in and really think about what you saw tonight."

"That'd be good."

He started toward the house then looked back at us.

"I think I'm dreaming. I'm not sure if it's good or bad yet." He glanced at the house then back at us. "Am I going to die if I walk into that house?"

"That house is probably the safest place in Uttira for you," I said.

"Megan is correct," Adira said. "Nothing can harm you in that house."

He nodded and started toward the door. Without a word, he unlocked it and slipped inside. Adira and I watched the lights go on one by one.

"I controlled myself in that alley. Well, before those three men showed up. There were at least twenty other people I could feel, and I didn't do a thing about it."

"But you did for Randall Walker."

"You heard them. He and his friends were way more wicked. There was no way I could have just let them walk away. I mean, that's my purpose, right? To punish the truly wicked."

"It is. However, a fully developed fury doesn't need to strike the wicked for a confession."

"Well, I didn't know that. Maybe if you'd told me, I wouldn't have hit him."

"Did I have to tell you how to use your mind and your eyes to pull a confession from them? No. Yet, you somehow managed to do that." She gave me an understanding look that made me want to throat punch her.

"I know this is frustrating for you," she continued. "But, to keep the world safe, you need to remain in Uttira until you learn who and what you are, and you are able to control your instincts."

She reached out again and put her hand on my shoulder. A second later, we stood outside my house.

"Good night, Megan."

Then she was gone again. I stood there stunned.

"I don't believe this shit. That wasn't even a test. She just wanted to know if Eugene would work. Fucking unreal."

The renewed scent of smoldering grass sent me inside where I wouldn't start things on fire.

Are you avoiding me?

I groaned after reading Oanen's latest text and flopped back on the couch.

"Why must you keep texting me?" I mumbled, already tapping out my next message.

If I'm avoiding you, I'm doing a poor job of it. Aren't you supposed to be paying attention or something?

I can't when you're not here. I worry about you.

You need more interesting hobbies. Now, pay attention to whatever session you're in.

I'd rather you tell me why you didn't come in today.

I already told you. I hate people.

Adira asked if I saw you.

Adira can go pet a honey badger.

Seriously, that woman could go sit on a pole. I refused to listen to her and her dumb rules anymore. The Academy was a joke and a complete waste of my time. I wasn't learning anything there. Nothing I'd actually use once I left this place. I was tired of playing games and planned to stay on this couch until I rotted. No more recruiting new humans. No more babysitting existing ones. They could all suck it.

I set my phone on top of the small pile of papers on the end table, not wanting to see Oanen's reply. Nothing was going the way it should, and I wasn't in the mood for anyone, not even him.

After waking up feeling just as angry as when I'd gone to bed, I'd resolved to find my mom myself. Since coming to Uttira, well over a month ago, I hadn't received a single bill in the mail. Not one. Yet, I still had power, cable, and a working cell phone. Those bills had to be going somewhere. So, I'd done a little research and started calling around to look for information that might lead to my mom's current address or phone number.

However, my super sleuth skills had nothing on Uttira's impenetrable closed network. Calling the cable company had redirected me to the grocery store. Calling the power company had redirected me to the grocery store. And, calling the cell phone carrier number within the app on my phone had…redirected me to the grocery store. The woman working the day shift there probably hated her life now after that third call. She hadn't been able to tell me anything other than the Council takes care of all the orphans in Uttira. Fat lot of good that did me. If I couldn't track down my mom from inside Uttira to call her and couldn't leave Uttira to find her in person, I was royally screwed. Without her help, I had no chance of controlling whatever the hell was going on with me.

I stared at the TV, not really seeing the rerun so much as just attempting to let my mind go blank. What more was there to do than wallow? Nothing.

However, each passing minute only increased the resentment and anger crawling under my skin. One show changed to another, but I barely noticed. I wanted to break the TV. Burn the sofa. Destroy the stupid house in which my mother had caged me.

The knock on the back door only fueled the anger skulking inside of me.

"There's no one home. Go away," I said without moving.

The door opened, and the faint scuff of footsteps announced the approach of my would-be visitor.

"I should have locked it," I mumbled to myself.

"No, you shouldn't have, or I would have broken it," Oanen said.

I lifted my head to look up at him and wished I hadn't. Scabs still clung to his face in a few places, yet another reminder of my failings. Setting my head back on the couch, I resumed my TV stare.

Oanen moved closer and squatted down beside me, blocking my view. It didn't matter. I kept my eyes trained on the blur of his bare chest.

"Talk to me, Megan," he said softly. "Tell me what you're thinking right now."

"That I suck at girlfriending, and the only thing I do well is hurt people."

"That's not true."

"Careful. I'm pretty sure lying is wicked."

"What happened last night?"

"Exactly what Adira wanted to happen. I verified the new human wasn't wicked then lost it when a group of drug-dealing thugs came over. My actions validated Adira's point that I'm a danger out in the human world and allowed her to refuse my request to leave to find my mom so I could get some fucking answers, which everyone in this seventh-ring-of-hell, shit-place likes to hide."

I took a calming breath and closed my eyes against the orange glow that reflected off Oanen's golden skin.

"You need to leave," I said.

"I've never needed to stay more."

"You're annoying me."

"Good. Then maybe you'll open those beautiful, glowing eyes and look at me."

I did, but it was for a full out glare.

His lips twitched slightly as I met his gaze.

"What are you most afraid of?" he asked.

"Hurting you."

"I don't think so. You've already hurt me. You feel guilty for it, but fear? No."

I thought about it for a second.

"You're right. I'm afraid of screwing this up."

"Technically, you already screwed this up."

"Is this supposed to be a pep talk? Because you're sucking at it. How did I already screw up?"

"You punched me in the face during our first meeting."

"I'm thinking about doing it again."

He grinned at me.

"How can you be so okay with all of this?" I asked. "I burn things when I'm angry. I can make people tell me all the horrible things they've done. My freaking eyes glow when I'm really upset. It's not okay. I'm getting worse. What's going to be next?"

He reached out and traced a fingertip down the bridge of my nose.

"Your eyes are glowing now, and they're breathtaking. I could look at you for hours if you'd let me. Do you understand? There's nothing about you that I don't like."

"You're crazy."

"Probably." He frowned slightly and removed his touch. "Do my eyes bother you when I change?"

"No." Dark blue or golden, his eyes did the same thing to my insides whenever he looked at me. But, I wasn't about to admit that aloud.

"I get what you're doing," I said, sitting up. "You want me to face my fears and make them seem less scary. It's not working. I fear myself. I fear that, whatever I become, will hurt you so badly that you won't heal. That you'll be dead because that's exactly what I think I was about to do to one of the men last night if Adira hadn't teleported me back here. Not only do I have no idea why I'm doing what I do, I have no control over it."

He considered me quietly for a moment.

"You might know more about yourself than you realize. Tell me about your mom."

"She dated a lot. Never really got attached to any of the men, though. Despite leaving me here, I know she loved me. At least a little. I remember hugs and kisses when I was small. I remember birthday parties before I started losing my temper and hitting other kids."

"Do you remember your mom burning things or having flaming eyes?"

"No. That's exactly why I need to find her. She knows what I'll become, and she knows how to control it."

"Her control means you will be able to control it, too."

"Before or after I fry the rest of the hair from your head?"

He sighed slightly.

"It's just hair. It will grow back."

"Speaking of going back," Adira said, stepping from a portal that spontaneously appeared in my living room. "I suggest you start where you left off."

She set her hand on my shoulder and sent me tumbling backward. I landed hard on my ass and grunted in pain.

"He said grow," I mumbled.

A bell rang, calling my attention to my surroundings. In disbelief, I glanced down the hall as several doors opened.

Adira had sent me to school in my damn pajamas.

CHAPTER NINE

ANNOYANCE EXPLODED INTO ANGER AS STUDENTS POURED from opening doors.

"Someone kick you out of bed?" a giggling voice asked from nearby.

What the hell had Adira been thinking?

I jumped to my feet and started toward the library, storming down the hall in my socks. Students moved out of my way as if I had Oanen at my side. Only, this time, it wasn't fear of him. They were finally seeing me for what I really was.

"Hell hath no fury like me," I said under my breath, trying to ignore the way some of the students called to me.

Adira had pushed me too far this time. I'd stayed home for several very valid reasons. One, the curriculum at Girderon Academy was a joke. This wasn't an institution for learning but endurance. And, two, I was running too short on any form of tolerance for anything. The students crowding the hall didn't help.

A boy left a classroom, stepping into my path at the last

minute. Had his wickedness been on par with Oanen or Eliana, I would have walked around him. Instead, I body-checked him without hesitation and smiled at his outraged yell as he fell. His backside barely hit the floor before I reached down and grabbed the front of his shirt to hoist him to his feet.

"Who do you think you are?" the boy demanded. I changed my grip from his shirt to his throat. He made a strangled noise, and his face began to turn red.

Another student tried to move in front of me. I backhanded him with my free hand, pushing him away, and focused on the wickedness coming from my victim.

"Francis Moss." My voice once again had that booming echo from the alley. "Conf—"

Something hit me from the right. The impact jarred me enough to loosen my hold. Thin arms wrapped around my waist, and a hand snaked up under my shirt. All the anger left me as I fell to the side.

My head hit the cement floor with a hollow thump. My ears rang for only a second, though.

"Don't let go of me," I said.

"I won't," Eliana promised in my ear.

"We have her," Ashlyn said from nearby. She continued talking, and I realized she was on the phone.

"She didn't hurt anyone...yeah, she's okay...Eliana, Oanen wants to know how warm Megan feels."

I just lay there and kept my eyes closed as if it would protect me from the reality of my life.

"Hot, but not burning me. She's cooling down already," Eliana said.

Ashlyn relayed the message to Oanen.

"He says he's on his way," she said after a moment.

A small groan escaped me.

"No. Tell him we're doing a girl's night," Eliana said quickly.

Snickering filled the hallway, reminding me that we weren't alone.

"Help me up," I said.

It felt like the entire student body of Girderon was trying to get a good look at the drama I'd caused. The kid I'd backhanded lay on the floor not far from me, shaking his head and blinking up at the ceiling. The boy I'd tried to strangle stood nearby, glaring but silent.

"Stop doing shit you shouldn't be doing, and I'll stop attacking you in hallways," I said. I pivoted and started walking, Eliana's hand still plastered to my back.

I'd only managed to clear the ring of gawkers when I realized I had no idea where to go.

"Which session is starting?" I asked.

"None. That was the final bell," Eliana said.

Adira had sent me here just to expose me to the students. Anger lit me from the inside again only to quickly disappear.

"Adira is such a bitch."

"Do you want to go home?" Eliana asked.

I immediately shook my head. I wasn't ready to face Oanen, who was likely still there with Adira.

"Want to come with us to Eugene's?" Ashlyn asked.

"Yeah, I'll ride along."

We took the back halls to the pool area before using the main hall to the parking lot. By then, most of the students had already left. Still, Eliana kept her hand on me, and

Ashlyn gripped her phone, most likely ready to speed dial Oanen.

The trip to Eugene's was short. Ashlyn pulled up in front of the house then looked back at me and Eliana.

"You two waiting out here?"

"Yep," Eliana answered.

As soon as the car door closed, Eliana removed her hand and turned to me.

"What's going on?"

It wasn't an accusatory question, only a concerned one.

"I don't know. Sometimes I'm fine. Sometimes I'm not. That guy in the hallway? His wickedness was way less than Trammer's, but I was still ready to kill him."

"I noticed," she said.

I exhaled heavily.

"Oanen thinks I can control whatever this is because my mom obviously did. But, it's getting worse. You saw his face."

"Oanen's right. If furies couldn't control themselves, they would be on the human news. There's got to be a trick to it."

"I'm sure there is. And I'm sure my mom knows. Too bad Adira has zero interest in allowing me to ask her."

Eliana set her head on my shoulder.

"I know you probably don't want to hear this, but I have faith in you. You'll figure it out without the help of your mom. Just like I'll figure out what kind of succubus I want to be without my mom's help."

I wrapped an arm around her shoulders and gave her a squeeze. It was so easy to get caught up in my own problems and forget Eliana had problems of her own.

"I'm sure you're right."

She lifted her head and gave me an understanding smile.

"I think this calls for some chocolate," she said.

"Good luck with that. Unless you have a stash at home, you won't find any at the store. I've been checking."

Her grin widened.

"You up for some more people time?"

The idea of going to her house made my stomach turn.

"Not really. Especially not anyone associated with the Council."

"That's perfect because where we're going, the Council avoids. Let's move to the front."

We did a seat switch, and she sent a quick text to Ashlyn, letting her know our plans.

"She'll text when she's ready for a pickup," Eliana said, handing me the phone.

She drove through town then stopped in front of a shop near the bakery.

"You should know that the lady running this shop is bringing in non-Council approved goods from the human world and selling it at crazy high prices to teens like us."

"Are you telling me she's wicked?"

"I'm telling you she's breaking Council rules. Personally, I think anyone who's willing to sell chocolate to a craving teen is as close to a saint as this place gets."

"The Council's rules are stupid. I've broken several, myself. I hope that isn't enough to make a person wicked."

"Let's find out," she said with a smile on her face as she got out of the car.

I did the same but with a frown. Fall's chilled breeze

swept over me. Now that my temper had cooled a bit, I felt every digit of the low temperature. Especially in my feet. Given the time of year, it wouldn't be long before snow covered the ground.

"I'm still pissed Adira didn't even let me put on shoes," I said.

Eliana glanced at my stockinged feet and grinned before entering the shop.

As soon as I stepped through the door, I could smell the chocolate. I inhaled deeply in appreciation and looked around at the homespun mittens, stockings, and hats hung on the walls.

"Can I help you?" the woman behind the counter asked.

"Hi, Mags," Eliana said. "I'm interested in the usual."

The woman glanced at me before answering Eliana.

"More mittens?" the woman asked.

"Gods, no!" Eliana said. "This is Megan. She's fine. We're interested in cocoa powder if you have it. If not, anything milk chocolate will do."

"Sounds like you have a craving," Mags said. As she spoke, anger threaded its way under my skin; and I reached out to hold Eliana's hand.

"Whatever you're thinking of doing, don't," I said. "Being wicked isn't healthy around me."

Mags grinned. "So, you're the new fury? I have some cocoa powder in back. Stock's low so I was going to charge double. But I'll give it to you at the regular price."

She shuffled to the back room, and almost thirty minutes later, we left the shop with not only cocoa powder but five pounds of sugar, too.

"Ready for some brownies?" Eliana asked.

"As long as we're talking the chocolate kind, yes."

We got into her car and drove to Eugene's to pick up Ashlyn.

"Please tell me that you convinced him there are better options," I said as soon as Ashlyn got in.

"I know you don't like it here, but for a lot of us, it's not a bad deal."

"You were almost drowned by a mermaid."

"And Eugene will escape gang rape if he stays in Uttira. He said he saw it happen to another boy his age. That's why he was sleeping in the cold by the dumpster in that alley. The men you saw, they only beat the boys."

"You know what frustrates me the most?" I said. "That there are people here who have the money and influence to make a difference, but they aren't. They're too caught up in their own petty problems."

"To them, controlling the creatures here is making a difference to the people out there," Eliana said.

Her phone beeped.

"Can you check that for me?" she asked.

I turned it over and found a new message from Oanen.

Where did you take Megan? I'm home and you're not.

"It's Oanen stalking me," I said.

"You better answer him," Eliana said. "You don't want him worrying and hunting you down."

"Unless you do," Ashlyn chimed in.

I rolled my eyes and started a text back.

"What are you saying?" Eliana asked.

"That you've tied me up and stuffed me in the trunk but were stupid enough not to notice I grabbed your phone. And that I'm running out of air."

"Don't send that!" Ashlyn said at the same time Eliana tried taking the phone from me.

I laughed at their reactions.

"Relax. I'm telling him to calm down his stalkerie, that we're on our way to my place to make brownies, and that he's not invited."

"You're making this hard on him, aren't you?" Ashlyn said with a grin.

"Making what hard on him?"

"Nothing," Eliana said.

I hit send and stared at her. When she didn't cave under my scrutiny, I turned to Ashlyn. She held up her hands and shook her head.

"She's my ride to school," she said.

"I'll drive you. Start talking."

"She means you're playing hard to get," Eliana said.

"What's to get? I already agreed to be his girlfriend."

Ashlyn snorted.

"Griffins don't do girlfriends."

Eliana slowed and signaled for my driveway.

"What does that mean?" I asked.

"Sweet mother Mary," Eliana said softly.

At first, I thought she was frustrated with Ashlyn saying something about griffins. Then, I noticed her attention focused on my car in the driveway. Through the back window, I saw the spidering cracks in the windshield. It looked like someone had hit the glass repeatedly with a baseball bat.

"What the hell?" I said, opening the door as Eliana parked.

The three of us walked to my car, all staring at the mess.

"We should call Oanen," Eliana said.

"No, we shouldn't. There's nothing he can do about this. Someone else might be able to help, though."

I went inside the house and picked up my phone from the coffee table where I'd left it. There was a message from Oanen telling me to text him when I got home. I ignored that and sent a text to Fenris.

Up for a favor? I need someone with a good nose to come over and tell me who bashed in my windshield.

I didn't have to wait long for a reply.

Will I be paid in spaghetti?

How about brownies? (The chocolate kind; not the ones with the wings.) We're making them now.

We?

Eliana and Ashlyn are over, I sent back.

Be there in 15. Can't wait for a taste.

"Um, who are you texting?" Eliana asked.

"Fenris. The Council's always getting his dad to sniff things out. So, I asked Fenris to come over and give my windshield a sniff. I promised to return the favor in baked goods, so we better get started."

"Oanen is not going to like that you called Fenris," Ashlyn predicted.

I waved off her concern. "I didn't call Fenris. I texted him. And Oanen will be fine with it. He knows that Fenris and I are just friends."

Eliana and Ashlyn shared a look before I strode to the kitchen. Having my car abused didn't put me in a good mood. Feeling like my friends were keeping secrets from me didn't help improve it.

"If you have something to say, just say it. All the looks

you're giving each other isn't helping the situation," I said, setting the mixing bowl on the table a little harder than intended. "Keeping secrets about presents or the Easter bunny is one thing. This feels like you're not telling me something really important."

Eliana shrugged sheepishly, and I knew she wasn't ready to admit what was going on. So, I looked at Ashlyn.

"I saved you. Don't make me regret it."

"Griffins don't date. They mate for life," she blurted.

I stared at her blankly for a moment. So they mated for life. Big deal. Why were they acting so weird about it? Then, it clicked into place. Oanen wasn't dating me.

Almost robotically, I sat in a chair.

"Do you think she's mad?" Ashlyn whispered.

Eliana bent in front of me so we were eye to eye.

"You're pale, which I'll guess means you understand. He made me promise not to talk to you about it. He didn't want you to worry."

"Why?" The word came out more of a croak.

"Griffin males are very protective of their mates. They care for them with a singular focus that's almost..."

"Scary?" I asked.

"I was going to say enviable. Succubi invoke complete adoration in their partners but rarely care for anyone more than they do themselves. Griffins aren't bespelled. Their adoration is their own. To be loved so completely by someone for what you are rather than some unnatural pull sounds like what love is supposed to be."

"I meant, why me," I said. "I was willing to give being a girlfriend a chance, but mate? I can't. My head feels like it's going to explode just thinking about it. How do I tell him no? I have to be the worst possible person for him to even consider spending forever with."

"Megan, just breathe."

I looked up at Eliana, who now stood by the kitchen door with Ashlyn. Both of their faces were flushed.

"Breathe?" I said. "You just told me Oanen already has me in a white dress in his head, and you want me to breathe?"

She swore under her breath, and Ashlyn fled outside.

"Megan, the heat coming off of you would be enough to cook an egg. If you don't want to hurt me, you need to calm down," she said slowly. "Focus on your breathing and nothing else."

I closed my eyes and tried. I really did. Only, once my eyes were closed, all I saw was Oanen's burned face.

The sound of the door let me know I was alone. I felt the first tear fall and wiped at my face, knowing it would be blood. It just made me more upset. What was wrong with me? Why was I so out of control? What the hell was Oanen thinking picking me?

The screen door creaked, and I opened my eyes to tell Eliana to leave. Instead, I saw Fenris.

He strode right up to me and wrapped me in a hug. I could smell his hair burning.

"Stop. You're going to get hurt."

"For the right girl, I'd do anything. Even risk my life for her best friend," he whispered in my ear. I jerked back and looked at him in surprise. His face was red and his hair a bit singed. However, no pain showed in his gaze.

"Feel better?" he asked.

I didn't know what to say or think.

Just beyond him, Eliana stepped up on the porch. Worry reflected in her gaze.

"I don't need brownies, just your silence," Fenris said softly before hugging me close again. He buried his nose in my hair and breathed in deeply. "Mmm. Her scent is all over you."

Eliana grinned big and wiggled her eyebrows.

"I told you so," she mouthed.

She didn't know. Like me, she had no clue. I wished I could go back to having no clue.

"You're getting warm again," Fenris said. "You're going to hurt my feelings if you keep thinking about him while I'm holding you."

I snorted.

"That's better. Now, do I have your word? She's not ready, and I don't want to upset her."

Since I wished I could go back to not knowing, I readily agreed with a nod.

"Good." He took one last, long inhale then stepped back from me. "The scent on your car is familiar. Someone from Girderon. I'll be able to give you a name tomorrow."

He leaned forward and, with a playful smile, licked the bridge of my nose.

"See you later, my sweet-tempered fury."

He turned and walked out the door with a polite nod to Eliana and Ashlyn.

"Is it safe to come in?" Eliana asked.

I nodded. Fenris had done his job and calmed me down by distracting me from my own drama. He was right. Eliana wasn't ready to know about his interest in her. Was it just interest, though? That thought led back to thoughts of Oanen as my friends joined me in the kitchen.

"Still want to make brownies?" Eliana asked.

"Yes. I'm sorry for losing it. Yet again."

"Don't worry about it," she said with a wave of her hand. "What are you going to do about Fenris?"

"Nothing. There's nothing to do. He's just a friend."

She rolled her eyes. "That's a lot of friendly hugging."

"I've kissed you. Do you see me as more than a friend?"

"Fair enough."

I sat in the chair and let Ashlyn and Eliana do most of the batter prep while I considered my situation with Oanen.

"I just don't see how this will end well for him," I said.

"Him who?" Ashlyn asked before licking some chocolate off her finger.

"Oanen."

"It'll be fine because you know you're meant to punish the wicked," Eliana said. "Just like I know I'm supposed to turn into a raving sex-addict and feed off the sexual energy of the thousands of poor souls I'll enslave in my lifetime. Who says I have to start now? Who says when you see wickedness you need to punish the person right on the spot. There's no timer for any of it, except these urges we get. So, next time, ask yourself why you need to rush it. Tell yourself you're taking your time to discover what the person did and even more time to weigh a suitable punishment. Be creative. Why let the gods have so much control even after they're long gone?"

What she said made sense. The gods had far too much control when they weren't even around.

CHAPTER TEN

I LIFTED MY HAND OFF THE BOOK AND LET IT FLY BACK TO ITS home on the shelf. My stomach growled as I stood and went to fetch the next one. Breakfast had been hours ago, long before sunrise.

Arriving at the Academy early had served two purposes. I'd avoided Oanen and given myself more time to look through the books. Fenris' revelation had opened my eyes to the value of knowing more about all the creatures here. So, while I hoped to stumble across a book that would tell me something useful about griffins, I no longer skimmed everything not related to my current topic of interest.

I still found most of what I read useless, though.

Taking the new book back to my chair, I opened the thin volume to the first page and started reading about harpies.

When I felt a cool breeze on my neck along with a mild tingle of annoyance that shivered over my skin, I remained focused on the book. When a heavy hand knocked on the door moments later, I ignored that, too. I wasn't in the mood to acknowledge Adira or face Oanen.

The breeze vanished, and the knocking stopped.

I glanced at the high window above the shelves. Plenty of daylight still remained. That meant it was lunchtime. Although my stomach voted for food, I voted for more seclusion. I needed time to just be me. Time to calm down so when I saw Oanen next, I wouldn't melt the rest of his hair.

Focusing on the book once more, I spent the next hour reading.

"Yet another race screwed over by the gods," I said, taking my hand from the book.

I stood with a stretch and grabbed the next one as I glanced at the window. Lunch would be over by now, and the next session in progress. I decided to stay another hour then bail.

My intentions flew from my mind when I opened the book and read the first line.

Like most creatures of the gods, griffins do not reveal the secrets of their existence lightly. The information contained within these pages has been documented at great personal risk. Make no mistake; if any griffin finds this book, any person known to have read these pages will be brought before the Council to have their memories wiped. Read on at your own peril.

James Whitenmore ~ 1927

Since Adira knew what was in the library, I knew I'd suffer little peril. However, as I turned the page and began reading again, I did wonder what had happened to the author since the book now resided here.

Griffins were created for a single purpose: to guard and

protect humanity against those creatures who would destroy us humans. However, there are not many griffins in existence. Their low population is perhaps due to all griffins being male. Based on my research, they are able to compatibly mate with any race. However, they only produce one male offspring with their chosen life-mate. Offspring are typically conceived not long after the bonding flight, the first flight for both the griffin and his life-mate, which they take together. A bonded pair...

I turned the page, eager for more, and found a blank sheet. Close to the spine, I spotted the jagged remnants of missing pages.

"Come on! Isn't censorship against the constitution?"

Releasing the book, I let it fly back to the shelf. I'd discovered enough to know I wanted to leave before the next session break.

I quietly left the library, collecting my things from the basket in the hall before scurrying down the empty corridors.

Outside, I went to where I'd parked my smashed car and found an empty spot.

"Smashing and now stealing?" I mumbled.

I lifted my phone, ready to message Fenris for another sniff-check, and found several missed texts from three of my four contacts. I read Eliana's first.

I told Oanen you know. Please don't hate me forever. He made me promise weeks ago. Please call me soon.

My stomach twisted with anxiety. Yet, I knew that Oanen knowing that I knew about the whole mate thing was probably for the best.

Closing her message, I opened the one from Oanen.

Saw your windshield and had someone pick up the car to fix it. I'll give you a ride home. We need to talk.

I growled and set off at a jog through the trees. Yes, we obviously had to talk. I just needed to postpone it for a while and give him more time to heal because I didn't trust myself to stay in control during that discussion.

More than twenty minutes later, I sat down on my kitchen chair with a relieved sigh and opened Fenris' message.

I know who it is. He won't bother you again.

The fury in me wanted to demand a name. I went for a brownie to shut her up.

For the next several minutes, I relaxed and composed a carefully worded text to Oanen so he wouldn't come looking for me when the final session ended.

No longer need a ride. Don't call me. I'll call you.

I hit send and leaned back into the couch.

"That wasn't so bad."

My phone immediately started ringing.

"Crap." I didn't touch the thing until the call went to voicemail.

A new text came through from Oanen.

I'm coming over.

The air around me started to smell like an overheated dryer. I quickly stood from the couch and sent him a reply.

Back off, fly-boy, or I'll rip your wings off.

I stared at the phone. Just when I thought Oanen wouldn't respond, a new message came through.

I'll see you tomorrow.

119

"So how long exactly do you plan to avoid him?" Eliana asked.

I propped the phone up with my shoulder and turned off the TV.

"It's only been an hour since I texted him. I wouldn't call that avoidance."

"You threatened to rip his wings off."

"He threatened to come over."

"That wasn't a threat," she said. "He's worried about you."

"Well, I'm worried about me, too. I almost toasted my couch."

"Seriously. It's only going to get more awkward. Just talk to him."

I stared at the dark TV screen. There was no denying how much I wanted to talk to Oanen. My insides went hot just at the idea of seeing him, of being near him. I wanted it so much. And that worried me.

"I can't," I admitted. "Not until his face is healed."

"You don't have to talk to him in person, you know. You do have a phone."

There was something about her tone and her persistence that gave her away, and I sighed in understanding.

"He's standing right there, isn't he?" I asked.

"He is," she said, sounding only a smidge guilty.

The phone became muffled as it switched hands, and my chest tightened in anticipation. How pathetic was I? I'd burnt Oanen so badly he was still sporting scabs, and guilt ate at my insides every time I pictured his face. Yet, I couldn't wait to talk to him or see him. Why couldn't I stop wanting him so much?

"I just need to know you're all right."

The low sound of his voice broke me as much as his words.

"I'm not," I admitted softly. "I don't know what to think, and what I feel is all over the place. I feel crazy and out of control. Why didn't you tell me that helping me off the roof would bond us? What if I don't want to be bonded? I'm not even sure I am ready for dating."

The one thing I did feel certain about was that I'd trapped Oanen into a relationship just like Aubrey had tried trapping Fenris. I angrily wiped away the moisture from my cheek, smearing blood across my fingers.

"Please don't cry," Oanen said. "The sound of your tears hurts more than any burn you could give me."

"Well, they aren't making me happy, either."

"Let me come over."

"No. Don't. I just need some time."

"You're saying no with your words, but I can feel your pain. Your need for me."

"You can feel me?" I said, freaking out even more. "There has to be a way to undo this, right?"

"This is why I didn't want Eliana to say anything. There's so much I need to tell you. Talking like this isn't helping. Please let me come over. If not tonight, tomorrow. You won't hurt me. I promise."

"No. I need more time. I'll call you when I'm ready."

I listened to his slow exhale, wishing he were right beside me instead of across town. I imagined his arms around me and another quiet tear fell.

"Don't make me wait too long."

TUESDAY, I woke early to the sound of my phone, which had remained quiet after last night's call. I lifted it and read the message from Eliana asking if I wanted a ride to the Academy since I had no car. I wanted to beat whoever had broken my window. That one act of pissiness put me in an uncomfortable position. If I said yes to a ride, Oanen would come with Eliana. I wasn't ready for that. However, if I said no to a ride and stayed home, Adira might zap my ass to the Academy. And, although I wanted to see if I could find anything more in the library about griffins, I didn't trust myself to keep my distance from Oanen.

I sent a quick text saying no to Eliana then another to Ashlyn, asking for Eugene, Kelsey, and Zoe's numbers. While waiting for a reply, I showered and dressed to ensure I wouldn't end up in the halls unprepared again.

When I checked my phone, I had a reply from Ashlyn, an acknowledgement from Eliana, and a new message from Oanen. I read Oanen's first.

I'll let Adira know you won't be in today.

That was it. There was no ranting or begging. Just Oanen taking care of me like he always did. Could he be any more perfect? I doubted it.

I sighed and sent quick texts asking each of the three new residents of Uttira if they needed anything and if they planned on attending the Academy. Kelsey and Zoe both answered that they were doing well but taking things slowly and didn't plan on attending until next term. Eugene said he'd be there Friday after he received his new clothes because he didn't want to look like a homeless drifter anymore.

Making a mental note that I would need to go in Friday, I looked around for something else to keep me busy.

I cleaned the house with a vengeance. Floors, that weren't really dirty, got swept and scrubbed, including the stairs. I dusted the bedrooms, washed the bedding, and de-webbed ceiling corners. In the kitchen, I washed cabinets and removed everything from the fridge before washing the inside of that, too.

By the time I reached the library, I only opened the door I'd shut long ago, gave the room a glance, and closed the door again. The sun had set, and I was exhausted.

I made myself a quick dinner then went to bed. I thought of Oanen as I closed my eyes and wondered if his day had been as boring without me as my day had been without him.

Thinking of him just before sleeping proved unwise. I dreamt of him flying around endlessly in a storm, searching for me. Lightning hit him repeatedly, burning his feathers and scorching his skin, but he refused to land and stop his search. When I woke drenched in my own sweat, it was because I'd witnessed him die from a lightning strike straight to his heart. It hadn't come from the sky, but from my hands when he'd finally found me.

I wiped my face and sat up, shaking. Sunlight already lit the room, not that the brightness helped ease the fear I felt. I'd killed Oanen. With fire.

I picked up my phone and hesitated. Sending him a message to ask him to let Adira know I wouldn't be in again felt mean. Yet, after that dream, I couldn't ignore the warning.

I won't be in again today. Maybe tomorrow, I sent.

A moment later, he replied.

I'll let Adira know.

How could four words convey so much sadness? Maybe because of my own misery.

I set the phone aside and went back to sleep.

After several hours, I woke again and got ready for another boring day. Since I'd cleaned yesterday, I decided to make a mess in the kitchen. Using the internet, I found a recipe for chocolate mousse layer cake and spent the next three hours baking then eating my creation. Chocolate had to have soul-healing powers because, after a few bites, life didn't feel as bad.

Before I finished washing the mess of dishes I'd made, the rumble of an engine reached my ears. Frowning, I grabbed a towel for my hands and went toward the door just in time to see my car come to a stop. A sheen of familiar golden hair flashed through the newly repaired windshield. My heart thumped heavily, and I stepped closer to the door.

Oanen got out. He didn't look up at the house, instead he kept his eyes trained on the car. He set his hand on the roof and closed his eyes, a look of anguish crossing his features.

An aching need twisted in my chest. I couldn't stand seeing him hurt like that. Even burned, he hadn't looked so tormented.

I opened the door. His expression immediately closed off before his gaze met mine through the screen.

"Adira says that I can't really hurt anything in this

house," I said, my heart beating faster. "It'd be better if you came inside."

He lifted his hand from the car and slowly stalked toward me. My pulse raced in anticipation and concern.

He didn't hesitate on the steps but took the door from my fingers and let himself in. I slowly backed away, keeping our personal bubbles intact.

His deep blue eyes studied me for a long moment.

"I never meant to hurt you," he said softly.

"You didn't. I understand why you didn't want me to know. I mean, I freaked out just like you'd anticipated, right?"

"Are you still freaking out?"

"Yes. My heart feels like it's trying to pound its way out of my chest."

"I know." He looked away for a moment. "But, I don't know how to make this easier, Megan. How to ease your fears."

"I don't think you can. Without knowing what I can do and how to control it, I'm going to keep being terrified that I'm going to hurt you."

"You won't," he said, stepping closer.

I immediately retreated a step.

"Your face is already red. I can feel my own heat, like there's a fire inside of me growing each second I'm with you. It's not anger. It's need. I'm so desperate for you it's insane. I want you to hold me, but I know what will happen if—"

He moved fast, closing the distance between us and wrapping his arms around me.

"Oanen," I whispered in warning.

"Don't push me away. I need this just as badly."

I couldn't push him away if I wanted to. We fit perfectly, and I melted against him, laying my head on his chest against my better judgement.

"You're going to get burned again," I said.

"Your burns hurt less than your silence."

His hands rubbed small circles on my back, soothing and comforting me. I lifted my head to look up at him.

"We need to talk about what's going on, though."

"What do you mean?" he asked.

I wanted to say "bonding flights" but could only manage to mouth the words.

"Stupid library," I mumbled. I set my head back on his chest and felt him swallow hard before holding me tighter.

"I'd ask what else you learned in the library but know you wouldn't be able to answer." His hand stroked all the way down my back. I liked how he touched me.

"How about you just tell me everything then?" I said.

"I don't want to upset you more."

I didn't see how he could.

"I'm not ready for kids, by the way."

His hands stopped moving.

"I know you're not. We're taking this at our own pace, no matter what you read in the library."

"Good. That makes me a little less freaked out. So what are we exactly?"

"Bonded."

"And what does being bonded to a griffin mean? You said you could feel me. Were you serious?"

"Yes. Just the strong emotions. When you're happy, sad, angry, hurting."

"What am I now?"

"Still upset."

"Probably because you're starting to smell like burnt toast," I said, lifting my head.

He let me go, and I took several steps back. His face looked sunburned, and I was willing to bet he had new blisters on his chest where I'd set my head.

"Don't apologize," he said. "Those aren't the words I want to hear."

"What do you want to hear, then?"

"That you're not giving up."

I knew what he was saying. He wanted me to tell him that I wasn't giving up on us and on learning to control whatever was going on inside me. That kind of promise was too dangerous to give lightly. So, I gave him what I could.

"As long as you're safe, I'll keep trying."

CHAPTER ELEVEN

LIFTING MY HAND, I STARED BLANKLY AT THE TABLE WHILE THE book I'd just finished returned to its place. Knowing about the magic of light and dark elves was interesting since I was now certain Adira was a light elf, but I didn't see how the knowledge could help me.

Eliana's words floated around in my mind. Adira had given me access to the library for a reason. Sure, she made it sound like it was for my liaison duties, but other than checking the wickedness of new recruits, I hadn't done much of anything. Adira had also admitted there was nothing useful about furies in the library. Why, then, give me access? What was I supposed to learn in here? That I was just one of the many creatures that the gods had created? That the gods created us on a whim to fulfil a myriad of purposes to fit whatever agendas had filled their minds? All I was doing was questioning the validity of our existence. If the gods were no longer here to fight over the humans, why were any of us needed?

Someone knocked on the door. Shaking my head to clear

the questions, I stood and answered the knock. Eliana grinned at me from out in the hall.

"Where's Oanen?" I asked. Since we'd agreed on taking things slow without me avoiding him, I'd assumed he wouldn't avoid me either.

"Flying already. We're meeting up at the Roost in thirty. That includes you."

I groaned.

"None of that," she said. "I know how you get when you're cooped up in that house too long. Being cooped up in this library is no different. You're my ride. Let's go."

Most of the cars were already gone by the time we reached the lot.

"How long ago did the bell ring?" I asked, getting in.

"Not long," she said, joining me. "I figured I'd wait a few extra minutes so you didn't have to deal with the crowds and me at the same time."

"Getting tired of tackling me?" I asked with a grin as I backed out.

"Not at all. Those moments are always the highlight of my day. I just thought you might be a little mad with me after..." She shrugged and looked down at her hands.

"I get why you didn't tell me, Eliana. It was the smart thing to do. I wasn't ready, and you were protecting me."

She snorted.

"No way. I wasn't protecting you; I was protecting my soul. I'd made a promise before I knew you and couldn't break it. Especially now that I know hell's real. For what it's worth, I think Oanen should have told you from the beginning. Keeping that kind of secret can ruin a relationship before it starts. I hope it doesn't ruin yours, though. I want you both to be happy."

Her words only made me feel a smidge of guilt about the secret I was keeping from her. No matter what she said, Fenris was right. Eliana wasn't ready to know about his interest in her.

"Me too," I said, staying on topic. "But I don't see how that will be possible if I keep cooking Oanen every time he's around me."

"Have you asked yourself why it's just him? I mean, you're fine around Fenris."

"Probably because I have zero interest in Fenris romantically."

She made a non-committal sound.

"I'm serious. And I'm positive he has no real interest in me." Before she asked how I knew that, I quickly changed the subject.

"Now, is it really necessary to go to the Roost? Given my instability, and how easy it is for my temper to go off lately, wouldn't a girl's night at home be better?"

"No. This is Oanen's idea. You're going to practice control. Oh, and he wants you to wear the dress."

I opened my mouth to tell her that wouldn't happen, but she spoke first.

"He thinks wearing it will be a helpful distraction. You'll be too aware of the dress to be overly aware of any wickedness." She shrugged as I pulled into my driveway. "He might be on to something. You were okay last time."

"Do you not remember the incubus I punched in the face? I was far from okay last time. No. No dress tonight. It'll put me more on edge, and I don't need that."

However, twenty minutes later, I tugged at my hemline as I sat in the car and wondered what the hell had happened to my determination.

"Thank you so much, Megan. It's a lot easier to dress like this when you're dressed the same."

I glanced at her dress, glad we weren't. She wore a floor-length lavender number with a side slit up to the top of her thigh and a v-neckline that exposed the valley between her breasts.

"I would trip if I ever had to wear that thing," I said, pulling out of the driveway.

"It's making me nervous that Adira's picking out my dresses now. This one isn't bad, but what about the next one?"

"Most girls would kill to have someone delivering dresses like that to their door."

"Not if the gifts were from Adira. There's always strings attached."

"What do you have to do tonight?"

"Just dance. I pulled a page out of your book and threw down an ultimatum when she told me she wanted me to feed on the crowd's sexual energy."

"Oh? What was the ultimatum?"

She gave me a sheepish grin.

"If they don't stop pushing, I'd call my mom and take her up on her offer."

"What offer? I didn't know you were still talking to your mom."

"Yeah. That's the only thing keeping her out of Uttira."

"Hold up. I thought she left you here. Abandoned you."

"Yes and no. Succubi don't have maternal instincts by

nature. That's why she left me with my dad. When she came for me, it was to bring me here where I wouldn't hurt anyone while she taught me how to fend for myself."

"Weren't you twelve when you got here?"

"You see the problem. She didn't. The Quills didn't, at first either. Twelve is old enough for most succubi. But it wasn't for me. Oanen saw that right away. He's the one who stepped in when my mom brought me to the Roost and told me to pick a boy to give my virginity to. Because of him, she let me stay with the Quills. Because of my phone calls and updates from Adira regarding my progress, my mom's staying away. If I ask, she'll come back and show me how a Succubus is meant to live, using every man, woman, and child in Uttira as her teaching instruments."

"I can see why the Council would want to keep her away."

"Exactly. I guess Mom's one of the best. She doesn't understand that I don't want to have a horde of willing servants to satisfy my every whim. Her words not mine."

"So instead of feeding on horny teenage boys since you were twelve, you've been starving yourself?"

"No. My mom wouldn't have stayed away if I'd done that. I do feed when I have to."

"How?"

"I'd rather not talk about it," she said, blushing.

Since we were almost to the Roost anyway, I didn't press for more.

"So how are you going to monkey-tackle me with that dress on?" I asked instead.

"With grace, hopefully," she said as I parked.

I grinned at her, and we got out of the car. The cold air

had us hurrying toward the door and the familiar thump of music.

Inside, people danced as usual while others congregated in conversation around the couches or on the second-floor balcony around the bar. Familiar faces glanced our way as the gust of cold air swept in behind us. Thankfully, I didn't feel any strong threads of wickedness in the crowd. I did, however, spot Fenris with his her-herd in the center of the floor. He winked at me and kept dancing.

"I see Ashlyn, Kelsey, and Zoe. Let's go say hi," Eliana said. She grabbed my hand and tugged me toward the back of the room. I didn't mind skipping the dance floor for now.

"Hey, guys," Eliana chirped happily. "Any problems?"

All three sat at the table. Each appeared to be reading a book. I knew better.

"None," Kelsey said without looking up. "Ashlyn's coaching has made a world of difference."

Ashlyn snorted.

"Coaching? What coaching? All I told you was to ignore everyone. And that it works better if you have something to pretend you're distracted."

"There was more than that," Zoe said with a roll of her eyes. "But she made us promise not to tell."

"Fair enough," I said. "Whatever keeps you guys safe."

Zoe's gaze shifted from me to someone over my shoulder. I turned and found Jenna standing there, looking much better than she had the last time I'd seen her.

"I just wanted to say thank you, Megan."

"For what?"

"Aubrey was a bitch. Not the good kind. Stopping her was the best thing you could have done for us girls and for the pack. And, having her away makes life much nicer. I just wanted to let you know we think you're great, even if Fenris spends way too much time watching you."

I smiled as Fenris came up behind her just then.

"Hey, Fenris. We were just talking about you," I said.

Jenna's eyes went wide, and she gave Fenris a sheepish look.

"All good things, I hope." His gaze slid over my dress before briefly flicking to Eliana and the rest of our group. "You girls look lovely tonight," he said, once again looking at me. "Any chance that you'll dance with me?"

"You know what? Dancing sounds like a great idea," I said. I held out my hand for Eliana.

"I think I'm going to sit this one out," she said.

"What? Why? We came here to dance."

"I don't think I had enough for dinner." Her gaze pleaded with me to understand. And I did. When she blinked at me, I could see a brief flash of inky blackness creeping into her gaze. She warned me once before that Fenris had way too much lust oozing off of him. I kept my shock inside as I realized all the lust was because of her.

"Fine, I'll do this one solo." I turned to Fenris. "Looks like you're stuck with just Jenna and me."

"I don't mind." He took my hand, and Jenna's and led us on to the dance floor. Jenna grinned before busting a move in front of me. I smiled and started dancing until Fenris' arms circled me from behind. He pressed close and inhaled deeply with his nose buried in my hair. Now that I knew what he was doing, I didn't mind it. However, I was pretty sure Jenna did, based on her expression.

I mouthed "sorry" to her, and she shrugged lightly.

A shiver of awareness ran down my spine as if I were being watched. I looked around the crowded room while still dancing with Jenna and Fenris. A t-shirt, like the ones that Oanen usually wore, fell from above. I looked up, and my gaze collided with Oanen's as he gripped the balcony rail with one hand. The blue lights reflected off his chest. It was an amazing view that I couldn't really enjoy because his eyes were golden and very angry.

I stopped dancing.

With a small jump, Oanen launched himself over the railing. His gaze never left mine as he fell, and his wings burst forth to slow his descent. He landed in a crouch, and his gaze shifted to Fenris, who stopped dancing behind me but still had his arm hooked around my waist.

"Looks like you're not the only one with anger issues," Fenris said, much too close to my ear. "Because of what you're doing for me, I won't hit back."

Before I could tell him to cut it out and let go, he pushed me into Jenna's arms. I turned in time to see Oanen's fist connect with Fenris' face.

"Oanen, stop," I yelled. He didn't. Neither did most of the dancers or the music.

I grabbed Jenna's wrist and pulled her off of me just as Oanen hit Fenris again. Jenna whined in protest but didn't try to stop me once I was free. Stalking up to my irate boyfriend, I lifted my hand and caught his next swing with my palm.

His furious gaze shifted to mine.

"Outside, now," I said.

He jerked away from me, grabbed his shirt from the floor and stalked outside. I followed close on his heels. As soon as the door closed behind us and the music muted to the point we could talk, he stopped. He didn't turn toward me, though.

"We need to understand each other's rules so you don't go around trying to beat up my friends all the time. I mean, are you going to hit Eliana the next time I kiss her?"

"You plan to kiss her again?"

"If she needs me to, yes." I stared at his tense back in frustration. "Oanen, this isn't going to work if you have so little trust in me. I was dancing with friends, not having sex with them."

"You sure? Because it looked like that was where it was headed."

I lost it. My insides flashed so hot I thought I'd boil alive. Instead, the car right in front of Oanen exploded into flames.

I didn't care that a piece of metal flew from the car and hit him or that the fire would probably burn him. He could fry for all I cared. I wanted him to hurt like he'd just hurt me.

I took a step forward, ready to spin him around and give him a five-digit present when something hit me from behind.

"Are you kidding me?" I screeched as I went down.

The anger didn't disappear all at once but in slow degrees. As soon as I was in my right mind enough to know who I was struggling to get off my back, I stopped and just lay there, cheek against the cement.

I closed my eyes, hating myself. Could I get any lower? No. I'd managed to get every one of my friends hurt tonight. I could smell Eliana's melted dress. Guilt and shame clawed at my insides and ate away at whatever remaining hope I had for controlling the fury growing inside of me.

Eliana pressed tighter against me, and her hand brushed over my head.

"Shh," she said softly in my ear. "I have you, Megan. You won't hurt anyone else."

The last of my anger left me as did every other emotion. I lay there languid in the nothingness I felt.

"Are you okay, Oanen?" she asked.

"Fine. Megan?"

"She's not injured on the outside. Inside, she's not okay. We better get Adira."

Something moved inside of me. I wanted to feel anger toward Adira but couldn't. It kept slipping away from me. I felt stifled and raw.

"Get off me, Eliana."

"I can't. I promised I wouldn't let you hurt anyone. If I let go, you will. And, I won't break my promise."

Again, any hint of the anger or frustration I wanted to feel slipped away, along with my will to shake her off and stand. I continued to lay there as someone called Adira.

I never felt the portal open; it was already too cold on the ground to feel a temperature difference. But I knew the moment she arrived anyway.

"Your parents are on their way, Oanen," Adira said. "You can get up now, Eliana."

"It'll be okay, Megan," Eliana whispered in my ear.

Her weight lifted off of me. Before I could move, a hand settled on my shoulder. My stomach twisted as Adira's portal shifted me from the cement to my bed. Suddenly laying face up, I was too disoriented to do anything as Adira leaned over me and kissed my forehead.

Darkness closed over my consciousness, smothering the rage that had once again been trying to consume me from the inside.

"Rest."

That word followed me into the void.

CHAPTER TWELVE

I WOKE AT FOUR IN THE MORNING WITH AN INSTANT AWARENESS of what I'd done the evening before. The vision of that piece of metal flying toward Oanen's torso filled my mind along with the smell of Eliana's burned dress. Guilt threatened to suffocate me.

"Please let it not be that bad," I said as I reached for my phone.

I had a message typed and ready to send when I hesitated. If Oanen was hurt and recovering, I didn't want to wake him. Yet, if he was awake, he'd likely be worrying about me. That was his normal mode of operation. I frowned and looked at the phone. If he was awake, though, why didn't I have a text from him already? Worried, I sent my first text followed quickly by a second.

Are you okay? Please tell me you're okay.

Please don't give up.

When there was no immediate reply, I told myself he was still sleeping and sent a text to Eliana.

I'm sorry about last night. Are you and Oanen all right?

Instead of hovering near the phone until she answered, I went downstairs to make myself something to eat.

Two hours later, dressed and ready for the Academy, my self-delusion had evaporated. Neither Oanen nor Eliana had answered me. That could only mean one of two things. I'd either hurt them both so badly that they couldn't answer me. Or, they'd both given up on me. I doubted the latter. While Oanen might want to give up because of jealousy, I couldn't see Eliana giving up on me for what I'd done.

After a twenty-minute internal debate over just going to their house, I drove to Girderon early and continued to worry about both of them. Ashlyn arrived not long after with Eugene in the passenger seat of her car.

"Hey, Megan," she said as soon as she opened the door. "I'm glad you're here. I was a little nervous about bringing Eugene on my own."

It clicked that Ashlyn had been at the Roost last night, and I hurried toward her.

"Have you heard from Eliana? I'm worried that I hurt her last night."

Surprise flitted over Ashlyn's features.

"Hurt her? How?"

"You didn't hear the car explode after I went outside?"

"No. After Oanen hit Fenris, Eliana saw you and Oanen head outside and followed you. She sent a text later, saying that you guys were all heading home and that Adira would make sure that we got home okay."

"I missed a fight?" Eugene asked.

I turned my attention to him. Not only did he now wear clean clothes that complemented his jet-black hair and dark brown eyes, he also looked happy.

"Don't worry. You're bound to see a lot more if you decide to stay here."

He laughed.

"It's already decided. I love it here."

Ashlyn rolled her eyes but looked amused.

"You haven't even had your first day of school," I said.

"Doesn't matter. Look at how clean I am. They can do what they want to me in there, and I would die happy because I never thought I'd be clean and warm again."

Another car pulled in. Red and glossy with three blonde heads mixed in with one dark one, I knew right away who'd arrived.

Fenris waved as he held the door for Jenna. I noted that he looked completely unharmed by the two hits he'd taken last night. The girls looked over Eugene with keen interest as their group joined us.

"Everyone, this is Eugene. He's new to Uttira." I looked at Jenna and the other girls. "Would you mind keeping an eye on him while I talk to Fenris a minute about last night?"

Jenna nodded easily.

"Sure thing. We'll make sure nothing eats him."

The other girls grinned and wrapped their arms through his. Eugene smiled widely and gave me a thumbs-up before allowing them to lead him inside. Ashlyn followed with a shake of her head.

Alone, I faced Fenris. He watched me closely, his normal, easy smile absent.

"I'm worried that I hurt Oanen and Eliana last night. Please tell me you saw them after we went outside."

A look of relief crossed his features.

"I thought you were going to tell me I needed to stop touching you," he said, his boyish grin returning.

"I'm getting to that part, too. First, tell me what happened after I left."

He shrugged his shoulders and sighed slightly.

"I didn't want to make things worse, so I stayed inside. I heard the explosion a few seconds after Eliana followed you two out. I tried to get outside along with half of everyone else in the Roost. By the time I pushed my way to the front, I caught a glimpse of Mrs. Quill stepping through a portal before it closed. You, Eliana, and Oanen were gone."

That didn't help ease my worry at all.

"You need to tell Oanen the truth," I said, ignoring the cars parking behind him. "He's jealous of you."

Fenris snorted. "If I told him the truth, he wouldn't just punch me in the face; he'd try to kill me. Griffins are protective, if you haven't noticed. The only reason he's not angrier at me for the attention I've been giving you is because he knows he has your heart. No, I'd like to leave things the way they are for a while."

"Fine. Then, no more hugs for you."

He made a face.

"Now you're just being mean. But, that's all right. I'll love you anyway."

One of the people walking past us started walking faster, no doubt looking to spread that bit of gossip.

"And to prove my love," Fenris continued, "I've been considering your problems and think I found a way to help you. How do you put out a fire?"

"It depends on the kind of fire. Why are you asking?"

He chuckled.

"I've seen the flames in your eyes and Oanen's burns. There's a fire inside of you. You're trying to control the burn, right? Try putting it out."

He winked at me and merged with the flow of students going into the building. I stood there, thinking about what he'd said and waiting for any sign of Eliana's car or Oanen's shadow in the sky. When the first session bell rang, I gave up and went inside in search of Adira. Her door was tightly closed as usual, but there was no answer when I knocked. Frustrated, I checked rooms until I found Eugene with Ashlyn. Seeing them safe, I went to the library.

Words drifted before my eyes but none of them stuck in my mind. Hours passed. No one knocked on the door, and the growl of my stomach grew louder. Giving up, I went outside and waited in my car until the final session bell rang.

The cars cleared the parking lot in droves. While I waited to find out how Eugene's first day went, I sent the same text to both Oanen and Eliana.

I'm trying not to freak out, but your silence is scaring me. Please call as soon as you can.

Not long after I hit send, Ashlyn and Eugene emerged from the building along with Fenris and his girls. They all were talking and smiling. A part of me hated them for their good moods. Why couldn't I be like that?

Eugene spotted me and jogged over to my car. Fenris and his girls kept going to their vehicle, but he gave me a small nod of acknowledgement.

"Hey, Megan," Eugene said. "I just wanted to let you know I haven't changed my mind. Thanks for introducing me to Jenna. She and her friends are great."

"I'm glad you like it here. Just don't forget what this place is, and be careful."

He nodded and went to catch up with Ashlyn, who gave me a wave as she got into her car. Feeling defeated and alone, I started to back out of my spot. My phone chirped. I slammed on the brakes and picked it up.

My eyes devoured Eliana's message.

I'm coming over as soon as I can. Don't freak out.

I read the last line twice. What did she mean by that? Why did she think I would freak out when I saw her?

Checking behind me, I finished backing out and sped home. Once there, I paced in the kitchen, freaking out despite her warning not to.

When I finally heard Eliana's car, I had the door opened before she even parked. I focused on her face as she got out. She looked okay. Sort of. She was wearing more makeup than I'd ever seen her wear before.

"You had to use makeup to cover the burns?" I asked. Fear laced my words.

"No," she said, hurrying toward me. "I didn't. Look closely. The skin's all good. Let's go inside before you set something out here on fire."

I nodded and went inside with her. She held out a hand, which I clasped before hugging her tightly.

"I was worried I hurt you guys so badly you couldn't even text me," I said against her hair.

"I swear I'm fine," she said.

"Oanen?" I asked as I pulled back to look at her.

"Hurt, but not badly. All stuff that will heal."

"What happened? Why didn't you guys call me?"

"A lot's happened. Let's sit down. I've got an hour

before I need to be back home."

I sat across from her and noticed how beautiful her eyes looked with dark mascara and eyeshadow.

"If you're not wearing makeup to cover something up, why are you wearing it? I mean, it looks great; it's just very different from what you usually do."

"The makeup ties in to my visit." She reached across the table and held my hand again. "After the car exploded last night and Adira returned you, she and the Quills decided Oanen and I were hindering your progress."

"They what?" My anger wanted to rear its ugly head but couldn't, thanks to Eliana.

"We're not supposed to see you for a while. Especially Oanen. They took away his phone and have forbidden him from leaving the house for five days. Once they know he can control his urges to see you, they will allow him to leave the house, but he's done attending the Academy until you receive your mark."

Here and there, heat caressed me from the inside only to disappear. The Council was taking everything from me. My friends. The only family I had now. Even though I couldn't feel my anger, I could feel the overwhelming sensation of being alone and trapped.

I tried to stay focused on Eliana as she continued her story.

"The Quills were supposed to take my phone away, but I promised them I wouldn't text you without permission. When I got your last message, I knew someone needed to tell you what was going on before you lost control completely. I used heavy makeup as a bargaining chip. A week of makeup for an hour to talk to you."

My hands shook. I lived alone in the house where my mom had abandoned me; yet, my life had never before felt so controlled and managed by others.

"I know you're angry, Megan. Oanen is too. So am I. We just need to prove to the Council that he and I have nothing to do with the speed of your progress. Honestly, they should know that already. Look at me, right?"

"You're walking proof that they're right. Because of me, you're wearing makeup. Don't you see? We're all pawns on a chessboard to them. They move us around to manipulate our actions and reactions to each other. Now, the Council is taking you and Oanen out of the equation. Since we know you two aren't hindering anything—I mean, look at how fast these new abilities appeared—we have to ask ourselves why. Why are they separating us? Do they want a certain reaction out of one of us? What do they hope to accomplish?"

I took a deep, slow breath and let go of her hand.

"You should go. Let Oanen know I'm thinking of him."

She stood and gave me another hug.

"I will. I'd tell you to behave but..." She lifted a shoulder and gave me a knowing grin.

"I'll give 'em hell when I'm ready."

She nodded and left.

For the rest of the night, I dwelled on the possible reasons behind the Quills' and Adira's decision.

I LOOKED at the phone number and hesitated to answer. Last time an unknown number had contacted me, I'd found a dead body in the alley of the Roost. While discovering that body had, ultimately, helped catch the murderer, I wasn't up for any super sleuthing today. After waking up to a yard full of snow, I wasn't in the mood for anything more than a day binge-watching TV.

The phone stopped ringing, but a moment later a text message came through.

We require your assistance. Please meet me at the Quills' in twenty minutes. Adira.

I tapped out a quick reply.

I thought I wasn't allowed anywhere near Oanen or Eliana. You wouldn't want to keep me from reaching my true potential, would you?

Her reply was immediate.

Of course not. That's why we'll keep the meeting brief. See you soon.

I growled, turned off the TV, and got ready. In less than five minutes, I was on the road.

"Maybe this is a test," I told myself. "If I do well, they'll let me spend time with Oanen and Eliana. If I don't do well, maybe they'll kick me out of their crap town." I grinned at that thought. Outside of Uttira, I'd finally have a chance at gaining the answers I needed.

"So, I either need to play this really cool or lose my shit completely. There can be no middle ground," I warned myself. And since the likelihood of them kicking me out was low, I knew I'd need to try to play nice.

When I reached the Quills' house, I parked in the neatly plowed driveway. As usual, Mrs. Quill opened the door well before I reached it.

"Hello, Megan," she said with a welcoming smile.

"I can't decide what's real or not with you," I said instead of a polite greeting. "I mean, do you honestly like me? It's hard to say when I'm not welcome in your home unless I can serve some menial purpose. Speaking of...what can I do for you today?"

I couldn't believe I'd managed to get all those words out while keeping a smile on my face. Oanen's mother's smile, however, had faded.

"We never meant for you to feel used or unwelcome. We're only trying to do what's best for both of you."

"Right," I said. "Because actually giving answers and guidance doesn't do anyone any good. Got it. Now, what was it I could do for you?"

"We have someone in the study we would like you to meet."

"Lead the way," I said, fighting to keep my cheery smile.

I followed her up the stairs to the familiar study where Adira and Mr. Quill already sat with another woman. She was petite, blonde, and only a blip in my wicked radar. She was also much older than any of the other recruits.

"Megan," Adira said. "I'd like you to meet Uttira's new liaison officer, Anne Regan."

I stood there for a moment, unsure what to feel. I hadn't ever really wanted to be a liaison. Yet, the idea of someone else keeping an eye on the kids I'd okayed to live here felt wrong. Mostly, I felt set up, again. It felt like they were trying to control me in some way. Or maybe my reaction.

"Anne Regan, did the Council tell you what I am?"

"I'm sorry, no."

"Don't be sorry. Be aware. I'm a fury. I've been told I'm supposed to punish the wicked."

"You are, Megan," Adira said.

"And yet, you stopped me, Adira." I focused on Anne again. "They say they have our best interests at heart. And those of the humans. I can't say I've seen much proof of that, though. Watch those in the Council closely. Stand up for the humans. And, don't ever let me find out you're doing otherwise."

I turned and started out of the room.

"Aren't you going to ask about Oanen?" Adira said.

"Don't toy with me, Adira. I'm young and inexperienced now, but I won't always be."

I walked out of the study and almost collided with a wide-eyed Eliana. She grabbed my hand and led me down the stairs.

"I heard," she whispered when we reached the front door. "I'm sorry they took that away from you."

"It's no big deal. They said it would be temporary. I better go. I don't want to get you in trouble."

She grinned slightly.

"After your parting comment, I don't think they're going to do anything to upset you for a while." She hugged me tightly. "I'll see you tomorrow."

I left the house with a heavier heart than when I'd entered. When I reached my car, I looked back and caught sight of Oanen in a third-floor window. He stood there with his hands in his front pockets as he watched me. I couldn't tell what he was thinking or feeling in that moment, but I knew what he needed from me.

"I'll see you tomorrow," I said.

A hint of a smile curved his lips, and I knew he'd heard me.

CHAPTER THIRTEEN

"MR. AND MRS. QUILL, I'VE COME FOR YOUR SON," I SAID TO myself, grinning widely as I put on my jacket. "I mean to do right by him and won't take no for an answer."

Obviously, I'd been watching too many reruns in the last twenty-four hours.

Last night, I had decided to wait until after lunch today before I returned to the Quills' home. My decision had been less about the time of day and more about the amount of time I would need to mentally prepare myself for the unannounced visit. All morning, I'd tried to come up with something clever to say when I got there. Something persuasive that might reverse their decision to keep me from Oanen and Eliana. However, I wasn't any closer to being prepared now than I'd been last night. It didn't matter. I refused to put off my visit. I needed Oanen.

I locked up the house and got serious as I moved toward the car. Mr. and Mrs. Quill would likely tell me to get lost. However, I hoped my comments to Mrs. Quill yesterday would at least get them to hear me out. It frustrated me that

I didn't even know the real reason they were trying to keep Oanen and me apart.

"Why is honesty such a hard concept for so many people?" I mumbled to myself.

I pulled out onto the road and hoped I wouldn't come to regret what I was about to do.

Fifteen minutes later, I parked in front of Oanen's house. He was at the window and watched me get out of the car.

"You could make this easier by coming out," I said.

He shook his head slightly then stepped back.

"Playing hard to get isn't attractive for any gender," I said under my breath.

There was no one waiting to open the door. This time, I had to knock and wait in the cold.

When Mrs. Quill answered, surprise showed on her face.

"Hello, Megan. I didn't think we'd be seeing you for a while," she said, inviting me inside with a wave.

"Yeah, about that," I said when I was out of the cold. "This whole forced separation thing isn't working for me. I'm here to see Oanen."

"I'm sorry, Megan, but I can't allow that."

"Oh, you can; you're just choosing not to. Perhaps, if you could tell me the real reason why?"

"We're concerned that your time together is hindering your progress."

"Progress toward what?"

"Control."

"See, I disagree. What's hindering my progress is any lack of guidance, like I said last night. And I would like to believe that you, Mr. Quill, and Adira are unable to guide me because you lack the knowledge. However, I've seen Adira's files and the Academy's censored library and feel pretty confident that you three are purposely keeping information from me. Do you know what some people believe?" I asked, already feeling my inner fury stir as it had done at home when I'd thought this through.

"Some people believe that omission is as great a sin as an outright lie. And, in my book, sinner means wicked."

I embraced the change this time and knew the moment my eyes started to glow.

"I'm tired of being a pawn. Of being lied to. The gods control enough of my life already. I'm not giving more control of it over to anyone else. The Council has two choices. Let me leave Uttira or keep me but leave me in peace."

A cold chill crossed my back, and I turned just in time to catch Adira's wrist before her hand could touch me.

She winced and pulled back quickly, cradling her burned skin.

"You should know not to touch a fury when she's angry," I said, my voice already taking on a deeper echo.

"Megan, you need to control yourself," she said calmly.

I smiled, and it wasn't nice.

"I don't think so. Controlling myself would benefit you, not me. I think I need to let go."

Adira paled, and Mrs. Quill quickly stepped around me to stand beside her sister.

"We were wrong to try to keep Oanen from you. He's upstairs," she said as she reached out to press a speaker button near the door.

"Oanen, you have a visitor."

I briefly wondered why they were giving me what I wanted so easily.

"I expected more from you," Adira said. "And far less attitude."

"Why would you think I would have less attitude given the way you've treated me?"

"Because you were raised as a human."

I snorted.

"Human teenagers have enough attitude that most parents wish there were late-life adoption options. Don't judge all humans based on what you see in Uttira. Don't expect far less attitude from a teenage fury. Expect more."

Mrs. Quill reached out and touched her sister's arm, and they both disappeared in a portal.

I looked up at the sound of footsteps on the stairs. Oanen walked down, his gaze never leaving mine. I crossed my arms and studied him. He looked burned, again, but not as badly as I had imagined. Just a red face and singed eyebrows. Nothing that would have kept him in bed.

My anger continued to rise. Not at Oanen, but at Adira and the rest of the Council.

"I have to ask. What hold did the Council have over you that kept you from coming to me?"

"My mark," he said after a moment.

Although I'd figured they'd been blackmailing him with something, I hadn't thought that. He'd never mentioned wanting his mark so much that he'd give me up for it. Hurt speared me.

"Why is your mark so important?"

He didn't answer until he reached the bottom step where he stayed at least fifteen feet away from me.

"Because of you. Your house is almost always vacant. Furies don't live in Uttira. At least, not if they can help it. And, from what I've gathered, no one else wants furies living in Uttira either. That means, at some point, you're going to get your mark."

I considered him for a moment, letting his words and his meaning sink in.

"And without your mark, you think I'd just leave you behind when I got mine?"

"Something like that."

"I don't think this bonding thing works like that. Less than twenty-four hours without hearing from you, and I was going crazy."

"How crazy?" he asked, his lips twitching.

"Like level-cities-to-find-you crazy or at least rip-off-Adira's-hidden-fairy-wings-to-find-you crazy."

He chuckled.

"You seem to have a thing with ripping off wings."

"Apparently. Must be in my blood."

"She doesn't really have wings, you know."

"Whatever. Am I cool enough to approach yet?"

He glanced down at my feet. "Floor's still trying to burn."

I looked down and saw the spreading scorch marks around me.

"If I go outside to try to cool off, will I need to come back in to save you again?"

"No. I think you've made your point, and they'll leave us alone."

"For now." I sighed and moved for the door. "I'll be back."

Outside, I walked around, having fun melting the snow and blackening the grass underneath. After I finished writing "Furies should not play with fire" on the Quills' front lawn, I knew I could go back inside. It had taken me three passes to get the word fire dark enough.

Smiling to myself, I jumped a little when I turned around and saw Oanen right there.

"My mom sent me out to tell you she feels you've suitably learned your lesson about playing with fire and can stop writing."

"She doesn't really believe I was doing this to punish myself, does she?"

"No."

I glanced at the house.

"I don't know much about this boyfriend-girlfriend thing, but I do know I'm supposed to get your parents to want to like me. I completely went the opposite way in there."

"Don't worry. They do like you." He glanced at my creation on the lawn. "Feel better?"

"Are we talking temperature or vengeance?"

"Both."

"Then, yes."

"Good." He closed the distance between us and wrapped his arms around me. I hugged him in return, relishing the feel of his hold. It seemed like forever since we'd touched, and I hadn't realized how much I missed it and craved it until now.

He brushed back a bit of my hair and pressed a kiss to my temple. The fire that had gone mostly dormant flared, and I quickly stepped out of his hold.

Fenris' question about how I would put out a fire echoed in my head again. I hated that I needed Oanen so much but couldn't touch him or be touched like I wanted.

"Are you free to leave the house again?" I asked.

"Yes."

"Good because I want to go somewhere and try something."

"That sounds scarily vague."

I grinned and led the way to the car. Once we were inside, I opened all the windows before starting the engine. I didn't trust myself to stay calm.

"Are you going to give me any hints?" he asked when we reached the main road.

"Not yet. If I think about it too much, it'll get hot in here."

"I'm intrigued."

His tone was making my insides warmer by the second.

"Cut it out."

I forced my thoughts away from what I was going to propose. When I'd come up with the idea at home this morning, I'd almost melted the fridge handle.

It only took us a few minutes to reach the Academy.

"Are we breaking in again?" he asked.

"If we have to but not to get into Adira's office. The pool this time."

We got out and tried the student door. It was locked. I led the way around to the side where I'd found the open window before, and we climbed through. This time no one floated on the surface of the pool.

"All right," Oanen said once he stood beside me. "Now what?"

"Now, you get in the pool."

I took off my jacket and put it on a chair. When I bent and started to take my shoes off, a huge splash echoed in the room. I glanced at Oanen's pile of clothes then his wickedly handsome smirk as he treaded water.

"I think I see where this is going," he said.

"Really? Because I'm not even sure where it's going to go." I unzipped my jeans and put them on the growing stack of my clothes. Oanen didn't say anything as I tugged my shirt over my head and set it aside. I couldn't talk if I wanted to. My hands shook. I was nervous about standing in front of him in my bra and underwear. But, more than that, I was nervous about everything going wrong.

I walked toward the pool and sat on the edge, sticking one leg at a time in the water. Steam hissed up around me at first contact. The cold water started pulling away the heat curling inside my limbs and the steam slowed.

"In theory, the pool should keep me from overheating because of the temperature control for the water creatures who normally use it. If it doesn't, as soon as you feel the water starting to warm, you have to get out so I don't slow boil you like a lobster. Deal?"

"Deal," he said. "Now get in so we can test your theory."

I took a deep breath to steady my nerves then eased myself the rest of the way into the pool. Oanen swam closer, an almost predatory glint reflected in his eyes.

"Relax, Megan," he said with a slight grin. "I won't hurt you."

He wrapped one arm around my waist and pulled me against his chest while he gripped the edge of the pool with his other hand. The feel of his skin against mine escalated the heat inside me. Steam rose around us in the barest wisps while the water of the pool worked to keep me cool.

"Are you okay?" I asked.

"No. You're killing me. Kiss me already."

I grinned and set my hands on his bare chest before closing the distance between us. I touched my lips to his hesitantly, paying more attention to how the contact was affecting me and the temperature of the water than the actual experience. Oanen didn't allow that for long. He licked my upper lip then gripped me tighter and demanded more.

Holding tight, I groaned at the touch of his tongue against mine. His hand moved over my back, a cool stroke over my heated skin. We parted and looked at each other.

"Still good?" I asked.

"The best."

His mouth claimed mine once more. The passion of it robbed me of breath and cautious thought. I clung to him, losing myself to the kiss. To the taste of him. To the feel of him. The water rose over my shoulders and climbed up my throat as he let go of the pool and wrapped my legs around his waist. The feel of his erection firmly pressed against my underwear brought in enough awareness that I broke the contact once more.

Oanen reached up to move a piece of wet hair from my temple as he treaded water with his legs and watched me with golden eyes.

"You are the most beautiful thing in my life. A perfection I never thought the gods could achieve," he said.

"You're not just saying that to get in my panties, are you," I said, already knowing the answer.

"No. It's not the truth because I want you; I want you because it's the truth."

I looked at him for a long moment, embracing what I felt for him.

"How have you become my everything?"

I kissed him softly, a gentle touch of my lips to his.

The soft melody of a song about love and acceptance wrapped around my heart and encouraged me to give myself over to the handsome, exceptional creature who wanted me for his own. I smoothed my hands over his shoulders and around his back, pressing my chest against his. He groaned into my mouth. The song threaded around us, coaxing us both to let our passion for each other free.

Oanen gripped my legs and arched his hips against mine. Pleasure tingled through me. The need to give and receive even more rose higher as we sank under the water, our mouths melded in a hot kiss that threatened to consume my soul. I felt his need for me. His desire to call me his other half. All that I felt for him collided and gelled together inside my chest, a ball of emotion so intense it burned to be shared.

I loosened my hold on everything I'd been too afraid to let myself feel and sent it straight toward Oanen.

Water exploded around us. I opened my eyes in shock as his lips were ripped from mine and, through the bubbles, watched him fly backwards. He hit the other side of the pool with so much force that I could hear the tile crack even under water.

I surfaced, not even close to out of breath, and

frantically swam toward him. He wasn't moving, his body floating face down near a ladder. I hooked one arm around him, just under his arms, and pulled him toward the edge, ignoring the ladder and heaving him out of the pool and onto the cement ledge.

The moment I was on my knees beside him, I pressed my ear to his chest. The beat of his heart and the rise and fall of his chest reassured me.

Sitting back on my heels, I brushed back his hair.

"Oanen?" I called.

His face was once again blistered. Most of his skin had some degree of burn. His hair hadn't melted, but likely only because of the water.

"Oanen, can you hear me?"

He groaned slightly.

"Ooh. Looks bad," a voice said from behind me.

I glanced over my shoulder in surprise at a green-faced girl swimming in the water.

"I think I hurt him," I said, trying to fight my panic. "He's not answering."

"Oh, that's too bad. Enjoy that kick to the face," she said before diving under.

I didn't know who she was, but I wanted to kill her. Oanen gripped my hand, his hold stopping me from jumping into the water. I turned back to him and found his eyes open.

"Are you okay?" I asked.

"Yes and no. I'd like to go back in the water and try again, but I think I'll need a few minutes." He spoke slowly, taking small breaths after every third word. He would need far more than just a few minutes.

"You want to try again? Are you insane?" I asked.

"For you," he said with a smile followed closely by a wince.

I felt sick.

"How bad is it?" I asked softly.

"I think I might have cracked a rib or two. Help me up."

"I'm not sure you should stand. Let me call—"

"Megan, I'll be all right. I just need a hand up so I don't hurt myself more."

I hesitated until he tried rolling on his side on his own. The pain on his face had me getting down beside him so he could use me as a brace to stand. Each wince that pulled at his features tore at me. I'd done that. I'd hurt him. Again. How many times was it now? I'd lost count.

As soon as he stood, I helped him around the pool to his clothes. Helping him put on pants was awkward. Mostly because the green-faced bitch kept popping her head above the water and openly eyeing Oanen's ass.

Once he had pants on, I quickly dressed as well. When I turned to offer to be his crutch, I found him already halfway through the window.

"You're going to kill yourself," I said, not sure if I should help him climb out or pull him back in.

"I'll be fine," he said. He lifted his leg over the windowsill and disappeared from sight.

I leaned out the window, saw him lying in the snow, and quickly scrambled after him.

"We could have used the doors." I helped him to his feet and guided him toward the parking lot.

"We could have, but then the new liaison would have needed to come here, and I don't think she's ready for a second round with you just yet." Humor laced his words, an attempt to mask the strain in them.

"Second round?" I asked, playing along. "That's sounds like I attacked her or something."

"She's afraid of you after just one meeting," he said.

"Good. She should be afraid of everyone here. She'll pay more attention that way."

"Or become paranoid."

I opened the passenger door for him and watched as he eased onto the seat. Either he was getting better at not wincing or he was hurting less. When he was settled, I closed the door and ran around to get in behind the steering wheel.

"I don't even know if this place has a hospital," I said.

"It doesn't. There's no need. We all heal fairly quickly." He reached over and set his hand on my leg. "I can feel your panic. I'll be fine. Please stop worrying. Give me a week, and we'll try again."

The fact that he'd gone from saying a few minutes to a week hit me hard.

"How?" I asked. "I don't know how to control the things happening to me or even know what will happen. I didn't even know I could explode fire like that. We're not getting into that pool again."

"It's not your fault."

"Isn't it? I took you to the pool. It was my idea to see if the water would work."

"It might have if the siren hadn't started singing."

"Siren?" I thought of the melody that had been in my head and the memory of the siren who'd tricked men into thinking she'd been stripping on line.

"I thought that didn't work on us."

"It normally doesn't because our minds are naturally more shielded when we're aware of the song. We were distracted."

"So the song worked? I want to kill her."

"It wasn't a her. It was a him. The mermaid in the pool probably talked him into helping her. I'm guessing she's the one who went after Ashlyn?" he asked.

"I don't know. I never saw her face. I only—" I swore.

"What?"

"I kicked it. Yep, that was her."

I pulled up before his house and parked the car. He put his hand over mine to stop me from turning off the car.

"I'll see you tomorrow." He brought my hand to his mouth and kissed my knuckles. "Thank you for an amazing afternoon."

He was breaking my heart with the devotion in his gaze. He could barely move without wincing and had blisters all over his chest and face. The skin around his waist, where my legs had been, looked like it had already started peeling. All the damage I'd done, and he was thanking me?

I swallowed hard.

"Bye, Oanen."

He let me go, and I bit my lip as he slowly worked himself out of the car. At the door, he stopped and leaned down just enough to see me.

"Say it," he said. "Say you'll see me tomorrow."

"I'll see you tomorrow."

His lips curved slightly, but the smile didn't touch his eyes as he closed the door. I watched him start toward the house. Before he reached the door, I rolled down my window. The cold air calmed my mind and helped me make a hard decision.

"Oanen," I called.

He turned to look back at me.

"I think we made a mistake. We both need to come to terms with the fact that, no matter how much our hearts are saying yes, our bodies are saying no. Try to stay away. I'll try to do the same."

CHAPTER FOURTEEN

THE IMAGE OF OANEN STANDING SHIRTLESS IN THE SNOW stayed branded in my mind all the way home. He hadn't called my name or tried to stop me as I'd pulled away. Instead, he'd sent a text before I'd reached the road. A text I still hadn't read.

I turned into my driveway and parked in the back. Resisting the urge to pull the phone from my pocket, I got out and made my way into the house. Only after I'd hung up my jacket and put my shoes by the door, did I look at what he'd sent.

Playing hard to get isn't attractive for any gender.

I groaned. I'd known it wouldn't be easy as soon as I'd made the decision that we shouldn't be together like he wanted anymore. Taking a slow breath, I carefully composed a reply.

I'm not playing hard to get. I've tried to be the girlfriend you need. It hasn't worked. I'm sorry, but this is for the best.

His reply was immediate.

A few burns and broken bones change nothing. You're still mine. I'll see you tomorrow.

Why couldn't he just accept that we were done? I typed out another reply, hoping he'd understand.

I think it would be best if I take a few days off. Some distance will help us both come to terms with this being over.

I thought I'd get another text, but the phone remained quiet the rest of the day. Even Eliana didn't text. I kept telling myself it was for the best. However, the ache in my chest disagreed and continued to grow until I could barely breathe.

Once the sun set, I crawled into bed, hoping that sleep would mute the regret and denial I felt. However, sleep didn't come easily. I tossed and turned, the corrosive pain creating a misery I couldn't seem to escape.

Exhaustion finally pulled me under well after midnight.

Tormented by dark, wind-swept skies filled with lightning and an eagle's cry, I ran endlessly. There was no safety from the cold, pounding rain. No winged harbor in which to shelter. I was completely alone in a world that wanted to destroy me. Lightning struck me again and again, until the only forward progress I made was on my hands and knees, crawling through the mud.

Then, the rain stopped. A hand ran down my back and soothed the pain raging inside of me.

"You've suffered enough."

The mud between my fingers changed to sheets. The bed moved, and I turned to find the one person I'd been searching for. Oanen settled behind me and wrapped an arm around my waist to pull me close to his bare, wet chest. I relaxed against him and let my heartbeat slow.

"I refuse to believe what I feel for you is a mistake," he said softly, his breath brushing my neck. "We took the bonding flight. There will never be anyone else for me. You're mine, Megan. It's time you come to terms with that."

I sighed and snuggled in. The storm inside me settled and didn't return to torment me while I lay within the protection of the harbor I'd so desperately sought.

I WOKE SLOWLY, remembering the feel of Oanen's arms around me. However, when I turned, I was alone in bed. Frowning, I got up and went downstairs. He wasn't in the kitchen and the bathroom door stood open.

"Oanen?" I called. There was no answer.

Making my way back upstairs, I recalled the vividness of my dream. Had Oanen been just my imagination, too?

My heart ached at the thought that he'd only been in my head. How was I ever going to keep my distance if I felt like this in less than a day? I wouldn't be able to stop myself from running right into his arms if I saw him in person. Which was exactly why I needed to get my ass moving and get to the Academy before he did.

When I reached my room, I stopped and stared at my bed, hoping he hadn't come. Streaks of blood painted my pillowcase and my sheets. I'd been crying in my sleep. A lot. I wiped at my face and felt traces of crusted blood around my eyes.

"So attractive," I mumbled as I started stripping the bed.

With the bedding in my arms along with a clean change

of clothes, I returned downstairs to throw my sheets into the washer and take a shower.

Fifteen minutes later, I flew out the door with a lunch in hand and got into my car. It wasn't until I was at Girderon's gates that I realized my mistake. Monday check in. I'd need to face Adira. After the big scene I'd made about them not keeping me and Oanen apart, I'd gone and broken up with him. I hated eating crow.

The parking lot only had a few cars when I rolled to a stop. I got out and hurried inside, wanting to get the meeting over with.

Any hope of avoiding Adira died at the sight of her open door.

"Come in, Megan," she called before I could back away.

I went inside and stood by the chair.

"I'm here. What fruitless task in the guise of education would you like to set me on now?"

"You're welcome to continue using the library."

"What? You don't want the out of control fury mingling with the masses?" As soon as the sarcastic words left my mouth, I realized I'd spoken the truth and laughed.

"What happens when I read every sorry excuse for information in the library? What stall tactic will you use then?" I asked.

"I'm hoping you'll have discovered who you are before that happens."

"Why don't you just tell me?"

She sighed, her pleasant façade finally slipping.

"Fine, Megan. You're a fury, like your mother before you. Does hearing it from my lips help you understand who you are any better than you did before? No, it does not. Knowing who you are is about self-discovery. You need to learn who you are from the inside. When you do, you'll have all your answers about who you will become."

"Who I am on the inside?" I gripped the back of the chair. "I gave you a glimpse of the real me yesterday. I'm a burning ball of rage. A fire burning so hot I will destroy anyone and everyone around me. And, do you know why I'm so angry on the inside?" I leaned toward her. "Because my mom left me here. Because I have to deal with dumbass answers from adults who think they know so much. Because the gods made me this way."

The back of the chair disintegrated under my grip. I looked at the ash raining down on the floor then met Adira's gaze. A hint of worry now resided there.

"Stop playing games with me. It won't end well for you."

I left her office and closed myself in the library where I hoped I wouldn't hurt anything. With hours to waste, I set to work and searched for hints of anything that might help me break the bond with Oanen. He wouldn't like my solution, but it was the only one I had. I'd tried his way, and it hadn't worked.

The room brightened as the sun rose higher. However, each passing hour brought no new, useful information. I ignored the knock on the door and was relieved when no cool air appeared after it stopped. My stomach cramped, and I slowly ate my sandwich while I continued to read.

The light from the window dimmed, the first hint of just how long I'd spent pouring over these useless books. The current one outlined the lineage of several creatures. I was about to lift my hand and let it return to the shelves when something caught my eye.

Many creatures descended from Echidna, known by mortals as the mother of all monsters. She possessed the beautiful face of a maid with the body of a serpent. From her, a multitude of offspring were born.

Her offspring were gifted with an ability to appear exquisitely human to lure in their prey before devouring the flesh so many crave. However, one of her children, the Sphinx, did not crave the flesh of mortals but their minds instead. Only the smartest survived her presence. Those males she took to her bed; and from them, the first of the oracles came to the world of men.

These rare creatures were much like their goddess grandmother, Echidna, in appearance and their demi-goddess mother in knowledge. They could foresee the past, present, and future. So sought after was their counsel that many perished in the wars of men. Those who remained retreated from the world of men. Like the gods, their existence has turned to myth in the minds of mortals.

I lifted my hand when the book went on to outline another branch. I didn't care about minotaurs; I cared about oracles. If they'd all retreated from the world of men, that meant one could be here in Uttira. And, she could give me real answers about what I'll become and how to control my rage.

I quickly left the library and grabbed my things. There weren't any messages from either Oanen or Eliana, which I thought odd given that it was close to five. I couldn't believe I'd stayed in the library that late. Making my way through the dark halls, I sent a text to Fenris.

You wouldn't happen to know any oracles, would you?

His reply came through before I reached the exit.

No, but I'll ask around.

It was already dark outside when I left the building. Not dark enough to hide what someone had done to my car, though. This time, instead of breaking the windshield, my hater had scratched the paint to hell. First the smashed windshield, then the bullshit siren stunt at the pool, and now this? Everyone in Uttira seemed determine to test the expanse of my anger.

Pissed, I took a picture of the damage and sent it to Fenris without any words. Whoever he thought he'd dealt with hadn't listened, or I had more than one hater, which was a good possibility.

Lights shone through my windows when I got home. Frowning, I turned into the driveway and pulled around back. The lack of a parked car made me suspicious, and I quietly got out and made my way toward the backdoor.

Through the window, I caught sight of Oanen at the stove. My heart skipped a beat, and my chest tightened. Even with what I'd found at the library, I knew it would be smarter to stick to what I'd said and send him away until I could figure out a way to control the rage-storm always waiting to explode from inside of me.

He turned slightly. Although his moves were once more graceful and his expression free of winces, the view of his still red face helped firm my resolve. Those fearful moments beside the pool had almost killed me. I couldn't go through that again.

I opened the door and stepped inside.

"I hope you're hungry for burgers. That's about all I'm good at making," he said.

"A burger sounds good." I took a steadying breath. "I thought we agreed that we should try to stay away from one another."

"No. That's what you want to do. I never agreed to it." He turned the stovetop off and faced me. "We took the bonding flight. There's no going back. You need to stop running and accept what you already know."

"And that is?"

He walked toward me.

"We're meant to be together. I know you feel it. This need to be close to me. To see me, talk to me, touch me." He lifted his hand and cupped my cheek. "I know it hurts when you try to stay away. And I know you're afraid you'll hurt me more if you don't." He reeled me in until my chest brushed his. "Stop denying yourself what you really want."

His lips settled over mine in a kiss that stole my breath and made my heart race. I threaded my fingers in his hair and gave in like he wanted, even if only just a few seconds. His hips pressed against mine, a contact too close to what had happened at the pool, and I pulled away. He didn't let me go far.

"Tell me you're done fighting us," he said, resting his forehead against mine.

"Probably not. Each time I hurt you, I'm going to try to walk away. I care about you too much to risk you like that."

"And I care about you too much to let you go."

"We're at an impasse then."

"For now. Ready to eat?"

I nodded, and he released me. He fixed two plates, and we sat together at the table.

"What are your plans for tomorrow?" he asked.

"Not sure. I really don't think I can handle another long day in the library."

"I bet not. I'd ask what you found in there that kept you so long, but I know it wouldn't do any good."

I opened my mouth just to give it a try, and nothing came out. He chuckled then grew serious once more.

"What are the chances of you letting me spend the night again tonight? I won't be in tomorrow—my parents asked me to attend a Council meeting—and I'm not sure either of us would like another twenty-four hours alone."

"So last night wasn't a dream?"

"No. And I'm glad you didn't hit me to test it. Anyway, I couldn't have stayed away from you if I'd wanted to. You were in too much pain."

I couldn't deny what I'd felt then or now.

"Yes. You can spend the night. You can help me make my bed, too."

"Already done in hopes you'd say yes."

My insides went hot and cold at the insinuation.

"You mean you want to risk sleeping with me in my bed, don't you?" I asked.

"I do."

I couldn't stop the fear that raced through me. What if I hurt him again? I reminded myself he'd managed just fine the night before. Maybe everything would be okay.

"Changing your mind?" he asked, softly.

"No. You can still stay."

The rest of the meal passed in a blur. Oanen took a shower; and while he did, I quickly went upstairs and changed for the night. When I finished, I paced.

One bad dream, one little slip, and I'd crisp him.

"And I'm pretty sure fried griffin doesn't taste like fried chicken, Megan," I mumbled.

At the sound of Oanen's chuckle, I whirled to face the door.

"You talk to yourself a lot."

"All the sane people do."

"People talk to themselves about how much they want to taste their boyfriends?"

My insides exploded with heat.

"It's okay, Megan," he said with a slow smile. "I want to taste you again, too."

The heat grew worse, and I could smell the wood under my feet.

"New rule. You can't sleep in my bed unless I'm already sleeping." I lifted my arm and pointed to the hall. "You're in the guest room until you hear me snoring."

"You don't snore."

"Then you'll be waiting a long time."

He grinned, pulled me close to give me a quick kiss, then left the room.

"You're hot, Megan. But, nothing I can't handle," he called.

I shook my head and crawled under my covers. The smell of smoldering fabric surrounded me as I tried to calm my breathing.

"Sleeping yet?" Oanen asked from the other room.

"Go to sleep, Oanen."

CHAPTER FIFTEEN

A NOTE AND A PACKED LUNCH WAITED FOR ME ON THE TABLE when I came downstairs. Although his thoughtfulness warmed me, I would have rather had him present. Waking up alone in the bed had been a relief and a disappointment at the same time. But, the dual dents in my pillow and lack of charred sheets had helped ease some of the disappointment.

Grabbing the lunch, I headed out the door. I had no plans to spend the day stuck inside the library like Adira wanted. The time for patience was done. I wanted answers, and I wanted them now. The school was full of people who had grown up in Uttira. One of them was bound to know something about oracles. I should have asked Oanen last night, but the drama of us had gotten in the way.

Eliana was waiting for me when I pulled into the parking lot.

"Just the girl I wanted to see," I said, opening the door.

"Me too. Oanen said that he wouldn't be here today. I'm excited he's finally giving me a turn."

"You know you can hang out with us, too, right?"

"No way. Eew." She scrunched up her nose at me.

"Why not?"

"With what you two are giving off each time you look at each other, do you really want me to turn into a black-eyed crush muncher and start feeding off my pseudo brother?"

"Point taken. Sorry I didn't think of that sooner. You should come over tonight. I'll tell Oanen to take a hike."

Eliana laughed.

"Like he'd ever listen. You're officially in bonded-male griffin territory. There's no way he's going to let you alone for any significant amount of time."

"He's gone now," I said with a wry grin.

"He is. And I'm betting you have something planned that will probably upset him when he's back."

"Not really. I just want to find an oracle."

Eliana shook her head.

"Do you even know what an oracle is?" she asked.

"Yes. Someone with answers. Who do you think would know anything about oracles? Like are oracles still alive? Where do they live? Is there one in Uttira?"

"Well, Fenris was a good place to start last time," she said.

A thread of annoyance wormed its way up my spine a moment before a laugh interrupted our conversation.

"Like wolf boy would know anything about an oracle."

I turned to look at the girl. Her hair was a familiar mermaid green, which I tried not to hold against her.

"And you do?" I asked.

She smiled, showing a sharp row of small teeth.

"I do. I know a lot actually."

I let my doubt show on my face.

"Okay. What do you know?"

A hard light came into her eyes.

"Oh, it's not going to work like that, sweet fish. You want information; I want something in return."

Her attitude was starting to annoy me.

"You took what was mine," she said. "I want it back."

I frowned. Confused.

"I haven't taken anything."

Any hint of humor left her expression.

"You took my human and kicked me in the face."

Anger lit inside of me. This was the same mermaid? The one who'd tried to kill Ashlyn, and the one who'd watched Oanen and me at the pool? I fisted my hand.

Eliana's fingers immediately closed over mine, and some of the building rage left me.

"What exactly are you saying?" I asked. "That you want Ashlyn back in exchange for information that you may or may not have?"

"That's exactly what I'm saying."

"You're sick in the head. There's no way I'm handing over a human. Ever."

"Suit yourself." She smirked and continued on into the school.

I glanced at Eliana.

"Are you going to need to wear me like a backpack today?" she asked.

"Maybe. How much do you weigh?"

She grinned but didn't let go of my hand as we started toward the school.

The loud rev of an engine and the spray of gravel had us

both turning in time to see Fenris pull up. He was missing his usual her-herd. He spotted us before he even turned off the car and waved for us to wait.

His easy jog in our direction caught the eye of just about every female still lingering in the parking lot.

"Ladies. This is a sight. Tell me there's more after the hand holding."

I rolled my eyes, and Eliana released my hand.

"There might be. Someone trashed my car again last night." I pointed at the long scratches.

Fenris frowned and went over to inspect the paint. He sniffed a few times and shook his head in disgust.

"It's not the same person. I'll find out who it is, though."

"Thanks. This time let me do some talking, will you?"

He grinned widely. "Only if I get a hug."

I opened my arms and wasn't surprised to find myself pressed chest to chest with him before I could blink. He stuck his nose in my hair, breathed deeply, and made a quiet sound of disappointment before pulling away.

I tried not to smirk as he took my hand and lifted it to his mouth for an old-fashioned back-of-the-hand knuckle kiss.

"You need to work on your hugging skills," he told me.

"Thanks for the tip. I'm sure Eliana will be happy to help me today, though. You just get me a name."

"I'm on it, my wrath goddess."

I grinned and watched him jog away. When I looked at Eliana, I found her watching me.

"What?" I asked.

"I think he's trying to cause trouble between you and Oanen. Oanen's going to smell him on you."

"As you pointed out, Oanen's not here today."

She shook her head, and we walked inside, joining the masses in the halls.

"So why do you need to know about oracles?" she asked.

"Because I'm tired of bullshit answers."

Eliana laughed.

"That's all everyone here does. Why do you think an oracle would be any different?"

She had me there. But that didn't change my plan. I asked everyone during our first session. Some gave me looks like I'd dropped a silent bomb in class. Some sniggered and smirked but said nothing. The second session wasn't much different. I even asked Professor Flavian.

"Megan, oracles are dangerous creatures. It would be a better use of your time here if you returned to your studies in the library."

"Nope. It wouldn't. Been there. Read that. I need answers, and no one here wants to give them."

"I'm sorry, Megan. I can't help you."

"You won't help me. There's a difference."

I walked out of the room and straight into Eliana.

"I heard," she said.

"It's really starting to piss me off. You want lunch?"

She gave me a startled look then quickly hugged me. I laughed and hugged her back. My frustration immediately faded.

"That's not what I meant, but I'll take it."

"Oh, you meant–"

"Now this is what I like to see," Fenris said from behind Eliana. "Can I get in on that?"

Eliana pulled away and gave Fenris a scolding look. "I think you've hugged Megan enough. She's with Oanen, and you know it. Stop trying to cause trouble."

He gave her his best boyish smile.

"Does that mean you'll give me a hug instead?"

Eliana shook her head and turned to me.

"Ready for lunch?"

Fenris winked at me over her head.

"I wanted to let you know that I haven't found the car scratcher, yet, and the word's spreading that you're looking for an oracle. I'm still keeping my nose and ears out for both."

"Thanks."

We left Fenris and merged with the flow of bodies heading toward lunch. Instead of going outside, we sat in one of the free rooms to eat our meals in peace.

"Seriously, Megan. What are you hoping to learn? Why an oracle?"

"First, I want to know if there's an oracle even alive. Second, I want to find out where said oracle would live if said oracle is alive. Finally, I want the oracle to tell me what I will become or how I can control my temper. Both, if the oracle is willing."

"I don't know much about oracles, but I do know nothing's ever free. You'll need to give something to get something."

"Your hugs are free. Oanen's protection is free."

"Nope. I take something from you with each hug. And, the bond is the price of Oanen's protection."

"What about your friendship? Is that free?"

"Nope. There's a price there, too. You now carry the stigma of associating with the succubus who can't feed."

"My stigma doesn't seem to bother Fenris."

"That's because he wants something. I just haven't figured out what yet."

I took another bite of my Oanen-made sandwich so I couldn't answer if she asked me anything. She didn't, though.

"How am I going to find out what I need?" I asked after I swallowed my mouthful.

Eliana shrugged. "Keep asking people, I guess. Word is spreading. Someone's bound to know something."

After we finished our lunches, we tossed the bags in the recycling near the door. A tingle of irritation ran up my spine, and my head whipped in the direction of the hall. Eliana immediately grabbed my hand. Neither of us moved as voices filtered into the room.

"She's asking everyone."

"I bet she is. Don't tell her a thing. That bitch owes me a human. She has no idea what she stepped into."

I recognized the second voice. The merbitch I'd kicked in the face.

"Why not tell her?" the first voice asked. "She'd never make it to the island without help."

There was a moment of silence.

"You're brilliant. This is far better than getting people to trash her car or trying to get her to fry her boyfriend."

If not for Eliana's hold, I would have flown out the door. Instead, all of the rage trying to pump into me slipped away before I could embrace it. Eliana held my hand until their footsteps faded. As soon as she released me, I ran out into the hall but found it empty.

Eliana watched me closely, no doubt trying to decide if it was backpack time.

"Where's the island?" I asked.

"There's only one lake. I'm guessing it's there."

The same lake where I'd kicked the merbitch in the face. If there was an island somewhere on that large body of water, I needed to find it. There were two ways to do that. A search by water or by air. Either one would take some time if I didn't know a general idea of where to look. The lake was beyond huge.

"I need to go back to the library. I'll see you after school," I said absently, already thinking of what I would need to do.

"Behave," Eliana called as I hurried away.

I took my phone from my pocket and started dialing Oanen's number. Before I reached the second turn, I heard Adira's voice and stopped. She was the last person I wanted to run into. I was still pissed as hell at her.

"I trust you'll do well when you choose to leave," she said. "Your parents and I understand that it won't be until the bond is settled between the two of you. But when it is, there's some important work we need you to complete."

"I understand," Oanen said. "I'll do what's necessary."

I frowned and stepped around the corner. Both turned to look at me.

Adira smiled slightly.

"I'll let you share the news." She stepped back into her office and closed the door.

"News?" I asked.

"That meeting my parents wanted with the Council? It was for my mark. I didn't know."

A bubble of excitement burst inside of me.

"Let me see."

He turned his head, and I saw a large trinity knot on the column of his neck.

"My mom had that on the inside of her wrist," I said. I couldn't believe that was the mark that would let us in and out of Uttira.

"Yeah. Location and size don't matter. You can choose both when it's time."

"This is perfect, Oanen," I said, stepping close and grasping his forearm. "You can take me to see my mom."

His expression shifted slightly.

"I can't. It was the one oath I had to give before they gave the mark. I cannot take you from Uttira until you have a mark of your own."

I could feel my insides start to heat and quickly took two steps back from him.

He reached for me like he was going to close the space again, and I held up my hand.

"Don't. I'm not even sure this is far enough."

His expression changed to one of hurt.

"I'm not mad at you," I said. "I'm mad at the Council. Why are they such assholes?"

"They're trying to protect the humans. Without control, you could hurt a lot of them."

"No shit. I could hurt a lot of people in Uttira, too. That's why I need to figure out how to control this. I need the answers my mom can give me."

I clenched my hands in frustration and glared at Adira's door. Furls of smoke started to curl up from the wood door.

"I can try to find her," he said. "Your mom. The Council never said anything to prevent that. Do you know where she might be?"

My gaze flew to him, and all my anger left me.

"Yes. I do." I texted him our last address. "I think she's still there. Maybe."

"Good, and I'll go right now on one condition," he said.

"Sure. What is it?"

"You go home and stay there until I get back. Eliana will check up on you."

"Done."

He stepped closer and wrapped his arms around me.

"We'll figure this out, Megan. Together."

When he nudged my head up, I didn't think why.

His lips touched mine lightly, sending a zing of desire straight through me. Heat gathered in my middle once more. His tongue swept against the seam of my lips, and I opened with a small sound of need. The heat pooled under my skin. I gripped his shoulders and stretched taller, needing more contact.

He kissed me like he would never see me again, and I kissed him back just as desperately.

When we finally tore apart, his face was red, and he had two scorch marks on his shoulders.

I cringed.

"Don't," he said. "I loved every second of that. The fire of your kiss does more than burn me. It lets me know what you feel is real. That I really am the one you want to be with."

"Of course you are." I couldn't believe he would ever doubt it.

"It's sometimes hard to tell when you always smell like Fenris."

"About that. He's promised me to secrecy, but I swear to you there's a reason for it that has nothing to do with his interest in me."

Oanen studied me for a moment then nodded.

"Thank you. I trust you, Megan. And I trust him because you asked me to. But, it's still not easy smelling him on you."

"I know. I'm sorry. I'll ask him again if I can talk to you about it."

"After I'm back. Hopefully, it won't take long."

I smiled and shooed him down the hall.

"Go. The sooner you leave, the sooner you're back. And the sooner I can stop giving you second degree burns every time we're together."

He gave me one last kiss and strode away. Excitement coursed through me at the thought that all of our struggles might soon be over. I couldn't wait to just hug him without worrying about hurting him.

It wasn't until he turned the corner that reality pooped on my rainbow. My mom had moved us often, and there was no guarantee that she hadn't moved again. What if she wasn't where I'd left her?

I sent off a quick series of texts to Oanen with all the prior addresses I could remember then went to the library. Even if he did find her, there was still no guarantee that she'd talk to me. After all, she'd left me here with no clue in the first place. I was tired of waiting. The information about oracles was a solid lead to get answers. And now, I also knew one lived on an island in the lake. Wouldn't it be smarter for me to at least research what I could and know where she was if Oanen didn't find my mom?

Researching in the library proved to be helpful for a change. On one of the lower shelves, there was a large book that had a hand drawn map of Uttira. The massive lake had a spell on it that reduced its size in the human world while maintaining its size within Uttira. It was easily half the size of one of the Great Lakes.

In the center of the water, the mapmaker placed a dot and called it the Isle of Woe. There were no other details and no other dots.

I headed out the door with the information and didn't bother going to any of the other sessions. If I wanted to get to the island without Oanen's help, I'd need a boat and some supplies. And a lot of real, practical advice about mermaids that I wouldn't find in the books. I picked up my phone from the basket in the hall and sent a message to Ashlyn.

Do you have time to come over tonight? Or could I come to your place? I have some questions about the lake.

Sure. I'd rather you come to me.

I'll be there by five, I replied.

Oanen would understand.

CHAPTER SIXTEEN

ASHLYN SAT ON THE COUCH AFTER OFFERING ME SOMETHING TO drink. She looked less sad now. The dark circles that had shadowed under her eyes during the first week following her uncle's death were gone. Yet, I still saw hints of sorrow in her expression. It would likely linger for a long while. I couldn't imagine how it must feel to be still living in this place after losing her family twice.

I took a seat across from her.

"I'm sorry we haven't had time to talk much," I said. "How have you been?"

"Good. Well, not good. But better. I like having Eugene, Zoe, and Kelsey here. Camil and I didn't talk much even though we were close to the same age."

I recalled the girl who I'd found dead in the dumpster and felt a pang of regret that things hadn't changed in Uttira quickly enough to help her.

"How are they adjusting, in your opinion?" I asked.

"Eugene is embracing all of this. Kelsey and Zoe are taking it in. I think they're still deciding what to do."

"I wish the Council would just give them enough money to improve their lives and let them go."

Ashlyn snorted.

"Your heart's in the right place, but all the money in the world wouldn't stop what would happen to them. They have no parents. No guaranteed safety net. No one to protect them from all the harsh things out there. After living here, you should know the human world that you saw isn't what it really is. There are predators out there that will feed on the forgotten and unattached."

A shiver ran through me, a nudge of anger that didn't really have a source.

"Are you okay?" she asked. "Your eyes just flickered orange."

"You're safe; but no, I'm not okay. The talk of predators stoked the fires that have been kindling inside me since your uncle's death. There's an itch to do something about all of it. But, I'm stuck here." I leaned forward slightly. "Do you know anything about the Isle of Woe?" I asked.

"No. What is it?"

"It's an island in the center of the lake. There's an oracle that lives there, I guess."

Her expression changed to suspicion.

"Who told you that?"

"I overheard some mermaids talking."

She shook her head.

"Don't believe anything they tell you. They will do whatever they can to get you into their waters. It's probably a trap."

"That's why I wanted to talk to you. You're my best

source of actual information when it comes to mermaids. What happens when they get you in the water?"

"I don't know. Previous humans, who've gone in, haven't come back. Ever."

It was the same thing that Oanen had said. My outrage poked my fury anger, but nothing happened.

"I need to get to the oracle. Do you have any tips for me?"

"Yeah, don't do it. As soon as you put a boat on the lake, the mermaids will try to tip it. You saw what happens when they get you in their water."

"And you saw what I do."

She studied me for a moment.

"You'll need some extra weight in the boat to make it harder to tip. Some weapons to deter them wouldn't hurt either. Probably a change of clothes. If it's any amount of distance, you're going to go in. More and more mermaids will swarm the boat, and they'll work together. The sheer number will eventually tip you over."

I thought about it and nodded. I wasn't human. Even though I'd been hurt the one time I went in, they couldn't seem to hurt me permanently. Was it a risk I was willing to take? I thought of Oanen's burnt face and missing eyebrows. Yes. It was.

"When are you thinking of going?" Ashlyn asked.

"Soon," I said. "Oanen's trying to find my mom. He already checked her old address, and she isn't there. Everything's gone. This is my backup plan. I need answers, Ashlyn."

"Whenever you do go, start out at dawn. They aren't as active. And, promise to text me before you leave. I won't try to stop you; but if something goes wrong, the Quills will need to know where to start looking."

"Fair enough. Just make sure to give me a full day before raising the alarm."

MY PHONE BEEPED. I tossed aside the kitchen towel and checked the message. My heart thumped seeing it was another one from Oanen. He had been updating me on the progress of his search for my mom over the last three days, and none of it had been good so far. Being apart from him for this long might have been tolerable if he were at least finding clues about where my mom might have gone. But he wasn't.

Each day, the need for him grew stronger, and I worried about what would happen when I finally did see him again. I felt so unstable inside. I needed answers. I needed Oanen so much it hurt to breathe. And, that worried me.

Struggling to stay calm, I read the message. It didn't bring any better news than the last one.

Cali is another dead end.

I wanted to swear. Instead I typed out a relaxed message.

All right. Thank you for checking it.

How are you holding up? Want Eliana to take you to the Roost tonight?

I'd been stuck in the house for days. Truthfully, I was going stir crazy. But the last thing I wanted was a crowd of people and thumping music. I wanted to get the hell out of this damn town and strangle my mother. But I couldn't tell Oanen any of that, or he'd fly right back to me.

The thought of seeing him made my heart race in excitement, and for the briefest of moments, I considered telling him to come home. The memory of his burnt face stopped me. So, I lied.

I'm doing okay. Just finished the lunch dishes. Not really in the mood for the Roost. Fenris would probably be there in all of his hugging glory.

I felt bad using Fenris as an excuse, but I didn't want Oanen to make a call to Eliana despite my reassurances I was fine. Hopefully, his suggestion had nothing to do with what he might feel from me and had more to do with how well he knew me.

I miss you. I'll be home soon, he replied. A second later, another text came through.

We'll do some more research and try again in a few days.

My heart started to race in earnest. He was coming home? I squashed the panic and kept my reply cool.

Sounds good. I miss you, too.

And I did. So badly that I wasn't sleeping well at night. Mostly because of dreams where I was burning down the town. Sometimes Eliana was in the way. Sometimes Ashlyn or Fenris. Oanen was never in the way, though. Even in my dreams, I knew he was gone.

I grabbed my jacket and locked up as I left. I'd held off on my plans for the lake in hopes that Oanen would find my mom. That hope was now dead. With Oanen on his way home, the time had come for me to get serious about finding the Isle of Woe and the oracle.

First thing I needed to do was check the boat I saw at the

lake.

The drive didn't take long. I managed to arrive just before dark. The boat I'd spotted on the previous trip to the lake still sat off to the side, buried under a few inches of snow. After I brushed it off, I walked around it, looking for holes. It appeared solid. There were oars and even a life vest under it.

I took a picture and sent it with a message to Ashlyn.

How sturdy is this boat?

Her reply only took a few moments.

It's sturdy. That's one of the rules. The mermaids can't sabotage the boat before it gets in the water. You're not leaving now, are you? It's too dangerous at night.

No. Not leaving now. I'm checking it for tomorrow. I'll let you know for sure when I leave.

She didn't answer.

I checked the boat one more time then got back in my car for the drive home. On my way through town, I picked up three times my weight in water softener salt. The clerk didn't say anything, but I could see the curiosity in her eyes.

When my house came into view and I saw a light, for a brief moment anticipation exploded inside of me. Oanen. He was home. The thought had barely formed before I realized how impossible that would be unless he'd suddenly developed the ability to open portals like Adira. Flying would take him a few days to get back.

Eliana sat at my kitchen table when I walked in. Her expression sent a bolt of fear through me. I stopped just inside the door, afraid that whatever news she had would upset me enough that I would hurt her.

"What's wrong? Did something happen to Oanen?"

She stood and put her hands on her hips, scowling at me.

"No, you idiot. Something's going to happen to you. What are you thinking, going out on that lake alone after what we heard in the hall?"

Relief coursed through me. The fire that had scorched in my middle didn't cool, though.

"You didn't tell Oanen, did you?"

"No, because I'm going to talk you out of it before he even gets here."

"That's why I need to do this, Eliana. I can see your face turning red and know it's not anger. It's the heat rolling off of me. What do you think is going to happen to Oanen when he comes back? He's going to want to see me; and no matter how much I'm trying not to be, I'm desperate to see him. Every time I think of him I get warmer. He won't stay away because he'll feel how much I need him. Do you see the problem? I'm going to cook him like a Thanksgiving turkey. I need to go to the lake. I need to try to get answers. I need Oanen to be okay when he sees me next."

She exhaled heavily and dropped her hands to her sides.

"I know. I just need you to be okay, too, and I don't trust those mermaids."

"Neither do I. I have a ton of salt in my trunk. Ashlyn said to weight the boat, and I figure I can throw it in their faces if they try to tip me."

"Good. We'll stop and pick up some vinegar tomorrow morning, too. It'll burn them like the salt."

"We?"

"You're not doing this alone."

The heat slowly eased up as I faced my friend.

"You're amazing, and I love you," I said.

She grinned and crossed the room to wrap me in a hug. All the build up from the week slowly faded away as I returned her embrace.

"You're going to make me fat," she said, her head resting on my shoulder.

I snorted.

"I thought I was empty calories."

She giggled. "You are."

When I was pleasantly drained, she pulled away.

"Did you eat dinner yet?" she asked.

"No."

While she and I made sandwiches, she asked questions.

"What time are we leaving? How long do you think it'll take us to get to the Isle? And what's the plan for when the mermaids get us in the water? Because, according to Ashlyn, that will happen."

I looked at Eliana.

"You're making my Grinch-size heart grow way too big. I love that you're willing to go with me, but you can't."

She started to frown, and I held up a hand.

"Hear me out."

"I'm listening," she said.

"Did Oanen tell you what happened at the pool?"

She shook her head.

"He didn't say where you guys went or anything when he came back. Just went up to his room." She gave me a sheepish look. "I could tell he was hurt and had new burns, though."

"Well, I took Oanen to the pool, thinking the water

might be the answer to me not burning him when we touch."

"I'm sorry it didn't work."

"It might have if the merbitch hadn't talked a siren into singing for us. Needless to say, things got hot. Whatever's inside of me just exploded out. It sent Oanen flying. I could hear him hit the side of the pool even under water. I can't even imagine what would have happened to him if we hadn't been submerged." I held her gaze, silently pleading with her to understand. "I'm dangerous. I don't want to be, but I am. If they get me in the water, I'll get mad. I won't be able to control what happens, and anyone in the water with me will get hurt."

"So that's your plan? Boil the mermaids?"

"I don't think it's a plan as much as a foregone conclusion. It's not like I've ever made myself intentionally hot. It just happens with anger and passion."

She flushed at the word passion but nodded.

"It makes sense. The two emotions are very closely related." She smiled slightly. "It makes you taste good."

I laughed hard.

"You pervy little succubus. I'm your personal fury snack shack."

Her smile slowly faded as we brought our plates to the table.

"What if you go in and you don't get hot? They might get close enough to hurt you. What if your furnace doesn't work when you're hurt?"

I shook my head as she took her first bite.

"First, I think my furnace works harder when I'm hurt. Second, if I go in, it's going to piss me off. I hate lake water.

It's gross. Once I'm in it, I don't think they'll be able to get close. At the pool, my heat dried me within seconds of getting out of the water. The merbitch was in the pool with us, but she never got close. I think it's because I made the water too hot around me. My heat will be my personal protection bubble."

She held out her hand.

"Phone please."

I gave my phone over and ate my sandwich as I watched her install an app.

"What's that for?" I asked when she gave it back.

"I'm still going with you to the lake. But I'll stay on the shore and watch your progress on my phone. That app will track you. You should probably put your phone in a baggie before you get into the boat."

She had a valid point.

"And we should probably pack you a lunch and something to drink," she added.

I LAY IN MY BED, quietly contemplating the hairline cracks in my ceiling while trying to ignore the faint scent of scorch rising from my sheets.

After Eliana called the Quills to let them know she planned to spend the night, we'd packed my provisions and sealed up my phone. With nothing else to do, we'd gone to bed early so we could wake well before dawn and head into town for the vinegar Eliana wanted me to take.

Even though there was nothing left to do at the moment but sleep, I couldn't stop thinking.

What if there was no island? What if what we'd overheard and the map in the library was just some big prank to get me into the water, like Ashlyn said? Or, what if the island was real, but there was no oracle there?

The scent of scorch increased. If there was no oracle, there'd be no answers. Without answers, Oanen was as good as stuffed and served on a platter.

A scuff of noise preceded Eliana's entry. She wore a long, white virginal gown that made me grin.

"You need to sleep," she said, shooing me over.

I moved over for her and she laid down on top of the covers, facing me. She reached up and stroked my hair. It wasn't skin contact, but I could still feel her pull my worry.

"Just until you fall asleep," she said softly.

I closed my eyes and drifted off within minutes. My mind didn't stop its tormented thoughts, though.

I searched through storm swept seas, looking for an island. What I found was something that made my chest squeeze with fear. A mountain made of red jagged glass rose up from the water. Waves crashed upon the spiked shards, and the water turned to blood. Without a choice, I drifted to the shores.

When I woke, I was alone and there was blood on my pillow. Enough to leave it more red than the cream color it had been when I'd gone to sleep. I hated that I didn't know what I was becoming. It fed the rage that was building inside of me. Even alone, I wanted to strike out at something.

Staying quiet so as to not wake Eliana, I made my way downstairs and checked the time on my phone. Eliana's alarm wouldn't go off for another thirty minutes. Needing some time to myself, I went to the bathroom in hope that a shower would cool me off. However, I caught sight of my face in the mirror and only got hotter.

Dried blood flaked on my cheeks and crusted on the skin around my eyes.

"If I ever see my mom again, I'm going to throat punch her for taking off like she did. This is bullshit," I said to myself in the bathroom mirror.

After a shower, which only made me feel marginally better, I dressed and went to make us breakfast. I slid the second omelet onto the plate just as Eliana came downstairs.

She smiled at me, looking much too chipper first thing in the morning.

"Morning," she said.

I rolled my eyes at her and set our plates on the table.

"What? Didn't you sleep well after I left?"

"Not really."

"I'm sorry. I would have stayed longer, but it's not safe for me to feed after I get really tired."

"No, it's okay. It's just being away from Oanen. Sleeping is getting harder. My dreams are so weird. Last night, I was dreaming that I was already out on the water looking for the island. When I found it, it wasn't what I expected. I was thinking a small bit of green land with sandy shores. What I found in my dreams was a mountain of glass covered in blood. I knew I had to go there and sacrifice myself to get the answers."

Eliana paled. "I don't like this."

"It's fine. It was just a dream," I said.

"I've only been here a few years, but I've already caught

on to something very important. Nothing is 'just' anything here. There's hidden meanings, hidden agendas, hidden everything."

"So you're saying I should wear boots?"

She shook her head slowly.

"Your dream, if it is something, won't be anything that obvious. Just be careful, and don't be afraid to come back without answers."

We finished up our breakfast and got to town to buy out their supply of vinegar with ten minutes to spare according to Eliana's timetable.

"We need to get that boat loaded with salt, yet," she said as she pulled out of the parking lot.

"The bags aren't heavy. We'll be fine."

She gave me a worried glance.

"It was just a dream," I said for the umpteenth time. "I shouldn't have told you."

"Yes, you should have. We're friends, and we don't keep things from each other, right?"

I thought of Fenris and felt a brief stab of guilt.

"Telling you only made you worry more. It didn't change anything else. And seeing you worry now is making me feel like a jerk."

"You aren't a jerk. I would have worried no matter what. And it did change plans, remember? If we get to the lake and the mermaids are already stirring, you're going to bail."

"Right. But Ashlyn said they are never up this early. When Trammer tried taking her fishing at dawn, the fish folk had complained that their kids weren't getting a fair chance. It'll be fine."

She exhaled hugely and nodded. However, she didn't look any less settled when we pulled into the parking lot.

We worked in silence to unload the car and carry the supplies to the dock. The moon barely lit our path, and the brisk wind had Eliana shivering within minutes. She didn't complain, and I didn't try to tell her to wait in the car. When we had everything ready, we team lifted the boat and carried it to the water's edge. The gentle waves lapped at the wood vessel, the sound seeming loud in the otherwise quiet, predawn light.

Eliana glanced at the water for a long moment. I did the same. Nothing moved.

Grabbing the first bag of salt, I carried it to the boat and ripped the top open. Bag by bag, we filled the bottom of the boat with almost four hundred pounds of salt.

"That doesn't seem like enough," Eliana said softly.

"It'll be fine."

She nodded and watched me put my bag with my clothes, food, water, and phone into the boat. When I finished, I turned to her. She was on me before I could blink, wrapping me in the tightest hug yet.

"Be safe and come back," she said.

"I will. I promise."

She released me and watched as I climbed into the boat. The salt crunched under my feet with each step, and the boat rocked slightly as I sat. The lapping noises of the water had us both looking out over the expanse.

We waited like that as orange slowly painted over the sky's pre-dawn blue. As soon as the sun broke the cusp of the horizon, Eliana stepped forward and put her hands on the bow.

"If you see anything, turn back," she reminded me softly.

I nodded and eased the oars into their holders. She nudged me out into the water, careful not to step into the lake with her last push.

Carefully dipping the oars in the water, I gave my first experimental stroke to direct the boat backward. It was a little awkward the first go and Eliana chewed on her bottom lip as she watched me. But, the second one went much smoother. The sounds of oars softly slapping the surface and the slight thunk of the things holding the oars in place were carried away by the wind.

Eliana lifted her phone and glanced at the screen before giving me a thumbs-up. She was tracking me, and I wasn't even ten feet from shore. I shook my head at her and glanced at the water around me.

The sight of a face just below the surface almost made me yip. The mermaid's green hair drifted around her face as she smiled at me. Beneath the surface, something zipped toward us from her right. From the corner of my eye, I caught more movement to her left.

Instead of focusing on what it was, I looked up at Eliana and gave her a quick wave and smile, doing my best impression of a girl in a boat not surrounded by mermaids.

In three more strokes, I passed the end of the pier and headed out into open water.

CHAPTER SEVENTEEN

My mind raced as I continued to place more distance between me and the shoreline. Eliana didn't retreat to the car but watched me with a sharp eye. As did the mermaid circling just beneath the gentle waves.

Were the mermaids going to wait for me to reach the point where I'd be unable to swim back? If that was the case, they'd be disappointed. I swam well, and like any other physical activity I performed, I didn't tire easily.

I glanced at the faces beneath the surface, again, then grinned at Eliana as if the waters were still clear. I didn't want her freaking out and calling the Quills, or worse, Oanen. The threat of a few mermaids didn't worry me. But the idea of Oanen finding out what I was up to and rushing back did. I couldn't face him like I was. I couldn't risk hurting him. No, this was better. I could face a few mermaids, no problem. I just wished I knew what they were waiting for.

Maybe, like me, they didn't want to involve anyone else and were waiting until I was out of Eliana's sight. Hoping that was the case, I kept rowing. My arms didn't tire as Eliana's form grew smaller and smaller, but I did get thirsty. Just before she became too small to see, I lifted the oars from the water and found my drink.

"Can she still see you?" a muffled voice asked.

I used the bottle to hide my mouth before I answered.

"Yep. She's looking right at me."

Laughing drifted up around the boat; and I took a long swallow, relieved that I'd guessed correctly. After a quick, final wave to Eliana, I picked up the oars once more and mentally prepared myself for what was to come.

As soon as Eliana disappeared from view, the first mermaid poked her head out of the water.

"That took you far too long. You have to have the weakest arms I've ever seen. Are you rowing or having mini seizures?"

I ignored her and kept my pace steady.

"Does she know she's rowing in circles?" a quieter voice asked. Several others hushed her.

This time I rolled my eyes. Did they think I was stupid? Not only could I still see the shore on the horizon, I could also see the sun. Since both had stayed pretty much in the same place, I knew I wasn't rowing in circles. However, the question did bring up a good point.

Rowing in a straight line was all well and good, but I needed to make sure I was rowing toward the general direction of the island. At least, as far as the map in the library was concerned. I pulled up the oars once more.

"Why is she always stopping?"

"She's going to drink so much that she'll need to pee. I don't want her pee in my lake."

The boat rocked slightly.

"Poseidon's trident! How much does this land whale weigh?"

Ignoring them, I checked my phone. My location dot on the map showed that I was barely off the shore. Leaving the app open, I resealed the phone in its baggy and set it on the seat in front of me.

This time when I went to stick the oar in the water, a hand reached for it. I jerked the oar and whacked the hand.

Laughing, along with some swearing, erupted around me.

I set to rowing again, watching the mermaids dart through the water. They made a game of swimming under the boat to bump it, making it rock continuously. I didn't have a light stomach so the motion didn't bother me. In fact, if that was the worst they had, I would have no problem reaching the island.

They entertained themselves like that for a time while I slowly made progress. Rowing might not have been tiring, but it sure was boring once the shoreline faded from sight.

No sooner did I have that thought than a set of hands grabbed the right edge of the boat and pulled down as the left side was lifted up. I immediately leaned to counterbalance and put the oars in the boat. As soon as my hands were free, I picked up my hard, reusable water bottle and hit the hands still gripping the edge.

A head came out of the water, and the mermaid with green-blue hair hissed at me, showing her tiny, sharp teeth. Her grip on the boat tightened as she started pulling herself out of the water. Reaching down to the bottom of the boat, I grabbed a fistful of coarse salt and threw it in her face.

She screamed and dove back into the water. All rocking stopped.

"Fun fact," I said, starting up my rowing once more, "although mermaids can live in ocean water, they can't tolerate direct contact with dried salt. And, wouldn't you know, I got a boat full of it."

"I hate her," a voice whispered from under the water.

"I told you," another said. "Don't worry. She'll get hers soon."

I checked the water on both sides but didn't see anything. That worried me more than when they were swimming around.

Focusing once more on the map on my phone, I rowed harder. The battery was doing well, but my progress made me worry that I'd run out of juice long before I reached the shores again. Or worse, that I'd be making the return trip in the dark.

The absence of mermaids didn't last long. Within an hour, the number of them swimming around me had doubled. Another hour doubled that number again.

However, during those next several hours, little else changed. According to my phone, I was only a quarter of the way toward the center of the lake. And, every new mermaid asked the same dumb questions.

"Where is she going?"

"She thinks there's an island."

"She thinks there's an oracle."

Laughter ensued the last comment.

"An oracle? She doesn't need one of those. I can see her future just fine. Dead at the bottom of our lake."

While rowing had initially worked well to exercise the

tingle of anger that kept trying to worm its way up my spine, the activity was losing its effectiveness. However, my white-knuckled hold on the oars didn't just indicate my slipping control. It also kept the oars firmly in my grip. I easily powered through the hands attempting to steal the oars and even managed to connect with a few heads with every heave.

The cursing and hissing grew louder as the surrounding water churned with mermaid tails.

Was hitting them mean? Not based on the anger crawling under my skin. They were planning something that wouldn't end well for me if they had their way.

"Don't you have anything better to do? Go comb your hair with a fork or something," I yelled, losing patience with yet another attempt to grab an oar.

"She did not just go there."

"Oh, yes, she did," I answered the unknown, underwater voice. "Take your chum ass out to deeper water and go sing to Sabastian or something. Just leave me alone."

A head popped up to my right, and I zeroed in on the girl's livid face. Seeing a real target fueled my temper.

"Did you just call us shark bait?" she demanded.

"I sure did." I jerked the oar and hit her in the side of the head. She went under like a stone, and I laughed.

Another head popped up near the end of the boat, killing my humor. Her hate-filled gaze locked with mine. The anger I'd been feeling now made more sense, and the smell of smoldering wood tickled my nose as I stared at the mermaid who'd made me blow up my boyfriend.

"You think you're so smart filling your boat with salt,

don't you?" She smiled, flashing her tiny, sharp teeth. "Your boat's sitting heavy in the water. Too heavy to tip. Good job, orphan."

I wanted to launch myself at her but held my ground. She was baiting me. Why?

"What do you want?"

Her smile widened.

"You know what I want. I want that human. But I'll settle for you."

I snorted.

"You couldn't handle me."

"Alone? No. But I'm not alone."

She swam within arm's reach of the boat.

"Do you know what the problem is with your salt-filled boat that's sitting so heavy in the water?" she asked sweetly.

I narrowed my eyes at her.

"It's heavy enough to sink."

Something small jumped at the back of the boat a moment before water started gushing in. I pulled the oars out of the way of grabbing hands and rushed toward the back as the merbitch disappeared under water once more. Grabbing the plug, I swiped the salt away from the hole and jammed the rubber back into its place.

I looked around at all the faces staring at me from a healthy distance.

"Sink me and that means I'm in the water with you. Ever heard of a fish boil?"

They twittered with laughter and dove back under the surface.

Returning to my place, I picked up the oars and started

rowing in the increasingly choppy waters with a ferocity that made them laugh harder. The scent of burning wood and hot salt grew stronger, and I struggled to control my temper. How did my mom do it? All those times I'd said something that I'd known would upset her, she'd never lost her cool. I frowned. Not true. When she'd broken her coffee cup that last day in our old house, I remembered feeling a flash of heat. Back then, I'd written it off as my imagination. But I now knew it hadn't been.

The memory was less than helpful in calming me down, so I thought of Eliana waiting for me on shore. I needed to focus on getting to the island and back before sunset. I didn't want to worry her. I needed to keep it together.

The plug at the back of the boat popped out, again.

"I swear to the gods I'm three seconds from jumping into that water," I yelled as I once again put up the oars and went for the plug.

The lake's surface lapped at the outside of the boat, only inches from the top now, and I had nothing to bail out the water-laden salt. They would sink the boat if they continued to push out the plug.

Something clunked behind me, and I turned just in time to see one of my oars disappear over the edge. Whichever bottom feeder had it, she tossed it away from the boat. It landed with a splash just out of reach.

I swore and lifted the other oar out of its holder. I knew they wanted me to lean over and try to grab for the floating one, but I wasn't stupid. I'd already witnessed what they would do in that scenario. Instead, I used the oar I had to maneuver myself closer to the oar.

The boat rocked precariously beneath me, and I

widened my stance so the mermaids couldn't knock me over.

"The movies got it all wrong," I said. "Beautiful, kind creatures who long to be human, my ass. More like overgrown piranhas with the mentality of a goldfish."

A hand rose out of the water, gave me the finger, then closed over the oar. I watched the floating wood move away rapidly and bared my teeth in frustration. The boat jolted under me, almost offsetting my balance.

"Do it," I called. "See what happens when you knock me in."

They laughed again, and I continued to use my single oar in an effort to propel myself in the direction of the stolen one. The boat's movement in the water was slow and jerky. What little progress I made vanished each time the bitch with the oar swam further.

"Are your arms getting tired yet?" a singsong voice called.

"Hop in the boat and find out for yourself."

Silence greeted me and my hair whipped in my face as I stared at the surface. With all the rowing and anger, I hadn't noticed the wind until that moment. What I'd thought was churning water because of the mermaids was actually stronger waves. Tearing my gaze from the threat-filled lake, I looked up at the clear sky. Clouds hugged the horizon to the north, but the sun hadn't yet reached its zenith. Good. These mermaids were doing everything they could to slow me down, but I still had time.

The boat jerked under me. My eyes flew to the plug, but it was still in place. The boat jerked again then started forward so suddenly that I lost my balance and fell. My back hit the edge of the seat. I winced and rolled to my side to get to my knees.

The wind battered my face and made my eyes burn. Staying on my knees, I reached for my phone to figure out which direction they were taking me.

To my surprise, the mermaids weren't speeding me toward the shore. Just the opposite. As I watched, the dot on my GPS tracker crept closer to the middle of the lake. They were taking me right where I wanted to go. I grinned.

The boat stopped so suddenly that I flew forward and hit my head on the other seat. I swore and lifted my face to feel for splinters. I didn't find any, but my fingers did come away with blood. Heat pooled in my stomach and boiled over into my veins.

"That's the second time, Merbitch," I said under my breath.

I stood slowly, watching the water around the boat, looking for their laughing faces. I couldn't see any, though. However, in the distance, I saw something jutting out of the water. My heart gave a jump, and I wanted to shout with laughter. The island.

Something made a sound near my feet. I looked down at the water rushing in. They'd popped out the plug. Lake water closed over my shoes. I looked up at the island again then grabbed my phone, glancing at the dot through the baggy.

Lake water rushed over the back end of the boat. Weeds and bits of who knew what floated in with it. I had no choice now; I was going into the lake.

I dove over the side, smoothly entering the water. It hissed and sputtered the moment it hit my skin. I could feel how terrifyingly cold it was for only that split second. Then, my heat took over.

Surfacing, I wiped a piece of lake debris from my face.

"I smell like fish!" I yelled, truly pissed.

The water steamed around me and nothing swam nearby. Further away, a few heads surfaced, just enough to see their eyes.

"You wanted me in the water. Now, come get me." None of them moved. I started swimming toward one, which happened to be in the direction of the island.

"Here, fishy, fishy, fishy," I called.

There was no laughing this time. The mermaid dove under the surface and did not reappear. I put the phone baggy in my mouth and started swimming toward the island. Within seconds, I knew holding the phone like that was a mistake. The taste of melted plastic clung to my lips as I emptied water out of the bag and tried to power on my phone. It didn't work. Giving up, I stuck the device in my pocket and set out once more.

Numerous times, I had to stop to make sure I was still on course. It wasn't easy. Without the phone, I had to tread water and bob in the waves, waiting to catch a glimpse of the island.

My anger didn't cool with the freezing lake water surrounding me. However, the amount of steam drifting around me did begin to decrease.

The closer I drew to the island, the bolder the mermaids became. They circled me, once again throwing out insults and taunts.

"Does she actually think that's swimming?"

"Mmm...can you taste her blood in the water? It's delicious."

"That's right, sinker. One arm in front of the other. Get yourself nice and tired for us."

"Do you feel that? The water's cooling."

They were right. As the island grew closer, I could feel the strain. I had never pushed myself this far before. Any activity I'd done, I'd only continued to do until I felt my anger ease. Even though my anger wasn't easing this time, my energy was flagging. Why?

It took a moment to realize the talking around me had stopped. When I paused to get my bearings again, I noticed the mermaids a distance behind me.

"You're almost there," Merbitch said. "Do you think you'll make it?"

Ignoring her, I turned and continued on. The sight of the rocky, barren island sent a shiver of disquiet through me. It was far larger than I'd anticipated, and its jutting rock formations created a towering skyline that didn't look so different from my dream. The island wasn't glass, though, or covered with blood. Maybe my apprehension was from all the dead fish skeletons I'd need to wade through to get to the shore. Could the place get any more disgusting?

My feet hit bottom, and I sagged with relief. Plodding through the waist high water, I purposely ignored all the floating fish corpses. Exhausted, I stumbled onto the rocky shore and sat heavily. I'd exerted myself more than I'd realized because as I sat there I shivered. I needed to get out of the wind, dry off, and maybe even powernap before starting my search for the oracle.

In the distance, a single head rose above the water.

Merbitch watched me with a malicious smile. She was probably thinking the same thing I was. I'd safely made it to the island, but how was I going to get back?

The smile on her face fled, and she dove underwater, leaving me completely alone.

I thought of Eliana and sighed. She was going to be so worried.

"Well," a feminine voice said from nearby, "this is a surprise."

CHAPTER EIGHTEEN

STARTLED, I LOOKED OVER MY SHOULDER. A WOMAN DRESSED in a white, flowing gown stood near a pile of boulders. She was beautiful with windswept golden hair and brilliant silver-blue eyes. A warm, welcoming smile spread over her features as I stared.

Another shiver ripped through me.

"Such a nice surprise," she said. "It's not every day I get such a lovely visitor. My name is Lucia. Can I offer you a drier place to sit and, perhaps, something to drink?"

I carefully stood and wiped off the seat of my pants. Sand and delicate fish bones fell away from my cold fingers.

"My name is Megan, and somewhere warm and dry sounds great."

"Warm," she said with a smile. "Yes. Warm is good."

She motioned for me to follow and disappeared into a space between two giant boulders.

My shoes squished wetly as I walked up the sloped beach to the boulder strewn plateau. The crevice between the rocks was tight, but I could feel the warm air flowing out and saw the soft flicker of firelight.

With some wiggling, I pushed my way through. The dim passage I found myself in wasn't much wider than the entrance.

"It helps keep the heat in," Lucia said from somewhere ahead, as if reading my mind.

I took a step forward and something crunched under my shoe. I squinted down at my feet but couldn't see anything in the icky darkness gathered around my legs.

"I apologize for the mess. It's not easy to keep a cave clean."

I continued forward, that feeling of disquiet growing. But, no anger.

The ground tilted down slightly for several yards before I came to a bend. The light flickered more strongly ahead. I stepped around the edge, thinking to see an end, but it was just more passage. I looked back, staring at the sliver of daylight I was leaving behind.

"We're almost there, Megan. A warm fire and some wine. If you're old enough, that is."

I turned toward the firelight once more, my shoes crunching on something with each step.

"Old enough? I didn't think those rules applied here."

Her gentle laughter floated back to me.

"I do try to respect all rules. Without them, our world would be complete chaos. No one wants that."

Something rolled under my foot when I placed my next step, throwing me off-balance. I spread my arms to keep myself from falling, and my palms connected with cold, slimy rock. A dank, damp smell heavy with bitter smoke filled my nose. Flinching away from both the smell and the rock, I removed my hand. The smell vanished.

The oracle's home was disgusting.

"Why do you live in a cave?" I asked, carefully moving toward the flickering light.

"There's nothing to build with on the Isle of Woe."

I frowned. She was right. There'd been nothing but rock and bones. How, then, was there a fire?

Another bend reflected in the light. Warmth wrapped around me, making steam rise from the cold, wet jeans clinging to my legs. I knew I was getting close. Instead of hurrying, I slowed.

My gut was telling me something wasn't right, but my fury temper was quiet. Not a whisper of anger. Sure, I was annoyed as hell that I was cold and wet and smelled like fish, but that had nothing to do with Lucia. Why, then, did I feel like continuing was the wrong thing to do?

"Are you coming, Megan? I just poured you some warmed wine."

Unsure why I was feeling weird about the place, I soldiered on and rounded the bend. Relief rushed through me that the space before me wasn't more narrow passage.

A fire burned in an open pit to one side of the large cavern. Thick smoke curled up toward the tiny hole in the ceiling. My eyes barely noted the flames that I'd followed there. Instead, my gaze was drawn to a large, wooden table that took up the center of the space. Its grain gleamed so palely in the firelight that it appeared almost white. Dark engravings decorated the surface, epic battle scenes showing men in loincloths and armor fighting on mountains and in valleys.

"It is beautiful, isn't it?"

Lucia's voice drew me from the mesmerizing images. She stood beside the table and pulled out the single, cushioned dining chair.

"Come. Sit. Rest yourself, and tell me why you're here."

I walked toward the table and the old-fashioned goblet blocking part of a scene that kept drawing my eye.

"I came to talk to you."

"Me? Why?"

I managed to look up at her.

"You're an oracle, right?"

She smiled softly and gestured to the table.

I sat with a heavy exhale. Until the moment when I eased the weight off my legs, I hadn't realized just how tired I was. It felt weird being so exhausted. I would need to remember swimming in hypothermic lakes the next time I felt angry.

"I am an oracle. The only one in Uttira at present," she said, motioning to the heavy goblet. I picked it up and felt her hand brush over my wet hair.

"You're so cold. I have another gown if you'd like to change."

I shook my head and brought the goblet to my lips. The metallic taste of the cup made me hesitate. A heavy feeling gripped my stomach, and I glanced at the fireplace just above the rim of the cup. The flames danced prettily from their source. Bones.

I set the cup down quickly but couldn't seem to focus on the source of the flames again.

"What's wrong? Don't you like wine? I can fetch you some water."

"No. It's okay." I blinked, trying to focus on what was feeding the fire. Had I really seen bones?

A jab of anger hit me right between my eyes. Before I could react, it was gone. I frowned and rubbed my eyes, having a hard time focusing on anything but the flames, themselves, and the table and the feel of her hand on my head.

This wasn't right. I looked at the walls but could only see a hazy darkness. Something was very wrong.

"Why are you living in the middle of the lake?" I asked.

"We are all meant to be somewhere, Megan. Where would you have me be?"

"In town. In a normal house."

"Easily accessible? No, my sweet treat. That's how wars start."

Sweet treat? I wanted to shiver at the words and decided it was time to start listening to my gut even if my fury temper was quiet. My gut yelled at me not to relax or rest, that I needed to hurry up. That I was taking too much time even though I'd just gotten there.

"So how does this work?" I asked. "My friend told me there's a price for everything. What's your price to answer my questions?"

Lucia laughed lightly.

"Your friend sounds very wise. Most people who come here think answering questions is my purpose."

"Isn't it?"

"Yes and no. Although I can see glimpses of the future, that's not the sum of my existence. We should be more than just our purpose, don't you agree, Megan?"

"I guess."

"Don't guess. Know."

"That's why I'm here. Because I don't know."

"Oh?" she said, her hand stroking over my hair again.

"I need answers. My mom left me, and I need to know why."

"Let the past stay in the past. Why she left doesn't matter. Your future is what you seek, is it not?"

"Fine. What do you see in my future?"

"I see you drinking your wine."

A tingle of frustration raced through me, and I knocked the goblet aside. A hiss resounded near my ear. I turned back to look at Lucia and caught a glimpse of something that wasn't Lucia. A wide mouth and scaled skin. Her face came back into focus, smiling kindly with golden hair falling prettily around her shoulders.

She touched my hair again, stroking the dried strands.

"What's your true form, Lucia?"

She jerked slightly.

"True form? What do you mean?"

"We all have true forms, don't we? That's why I'm here. I need to know mine. I need to know what I'll become."

"Become. You'll become nothing more than what you are, cod fish," she said. Her hand left my hair, and she moved toward the fire. "I have some bread warmed, if you'd like."

She reached for something from the darkness near the pot. As she walked toward me again, her eyes reflected silver, like they'd caught light. But, she had her back to the fire.

Rage ripped through me, so harsh it felt as if I was going to be torn in half. I stood suddenly, knocking over the chair and slammed my hands down on the table before me. The scent of fresh wood smoke teased my nose.

The oracle stopped walking, the form of her face flickering ever so briefly between snake and woman at the same time my rage vanished. We stared at each other for a long moment.

"You are not what you seem," I said. "And, this place isn't what it seems." As I spoke, I looked around the room again. This time, I saw more than I wanted to.

A waist high ledge made of bones ran the circumference of the room. The floor was covered with them as well. They weren't human, but they weren't fish either.

"Are you eating mermaids?" I asked, dragging my gaze back to her.

She smiled slightly.

"You've already noted that there's nothing on this island. What did you think I ate?"

"I don't understand," I said, frowning.

She laughed.

"Of course you don't. If you did, you wouldn't be here."

Another jolt of anger poked at me only to vanish again.

"What I don't understand is why I'm not hurting you. Killing is wrong."

"My sweet fledgling fury, what defines wrong but the rules we are taught?"

My skin warmed with my growing irritation. She was responding to my questions with half answers and vague counter-questions. Although the swim in the lake had worn me down for a bit, my general pissiness was more than ready to bounce back.

The scent of fresh wood smoke grew stronger, and her gaze dipped to her table.

"Stop," she commanded, rushing forward. "You'll destroy it."

Smoke curled up from the table. My hair tickled my cheek as I lifted my hands from the wood and looked down at the scorch marks. The carvings that had been under my palm were gone.

"Hateful, hell bird," she hissed.

"Lying snake," I said, looking up at her.

Her gaze narrowed on me.

"I don't lie."

"How do you explain these bones?" I asked. "You're killing people, and I think I even see a few human bones over there."

"I've already answered that. I must eat."

"And, why am I not angry? Consuming flesh is against the rules. Wicked."

"Because the past does not exist here. Nor the future. Only the present. And, in the present, I haven't killed anyone or consumed anything."

Her words worried me. Not the killing, but about the time. Something was wrong with what had been happening since I'd arrived. My hair had dried while she'd touched it. Only minutes had passed yet my hair, which took a good hour to air dry, was no longer wet. My gut told me again that I needed to hurry up and get my answers then leave.

"What is my true form, and how do I control my rage?" I asked.

She smiled and reached out to touch my hair. I batted her hand away. Now, the touch of her skin against mine sent a shudder of revulsion through me. She felt cold and damp, like the stones.

Impatience stoked the fire growing inside of me.

"Lucia, you have about ten seconds to start giving me some real answers before I get really mad."

She laughed.

"I've done nothing for you to label me wicked, my tidbit."

I shivered at the words. If she wasn't doing something wrong, now, she definitely had something wicked planned for me in the future. Since getting angry at her wasn't working well, I went another route.

I focused on the flames licking me from the inside and thought of Eliana waiting for me and her worry. Then, I thought of Oanen. Of all the times I'd burned him because I didn't know what I was doing. Finally, I thought of my mom and all the answers she hadn't shared.

My anger climbed higher, and I knew the moment the oracle understood the situation. Her silver eyes reflected the orange light glowing from mine.

"If you leave now," she said, "I'll give you the answers you seek."

"No." I set one of my hands on the table and smiled. "Smells like toasting marshmallows, don't you think?"

"Hateful hell brat. I'll answer one now and one when you're in the boat, rowing away."

"Fair enough. But, I will turn around and destroy everything on this desolate rock you call home if you go back on your word."

She nodded and looked pointedly at my hand. I lifted it from the table and arched a brow.

"Come." She turned and started toward the crack in the rocks. "Your true form is born of—"

She disappeared from view, and I rushed forward, slipping into the passage.

"Born of what?" I asked.

"Born of fire. Keep up. I won't repeat myself. That is not part of our bargain."

I hurried, slipping and sliding over the bone littered floor.

"Vague answers aren't part of the bargain, either. I already know I have fire. I want to know my true form. What will I look like? Am I going to be a snake woman like you? I want specifics."

She laughed from somewhere ahead, the howl of the wind almost carrying the sound away.

"You are nothing like me. That you are born of fire means you are made from the flames of hell. You are hell's messenger. You bring the souls of the damned to their final place of unrest."

"But what will I look like?"

I turned the second bend and could see a dim sliver of light ahead but no Lucia. Another shiver ripped through me as the first gust of cold air rushed into the passage and hit my slightly damp jeans. It wasn't until I stepped out of the opening, into a wind lashed early twilight, that I understood what had happened.

Time had passed while I'd been in the cave. More time than I'd anticipated. A storm had rolled in, blotting out the light of day and turning the lake into a sea of crashing waves.

Ahead, on the shore, Lucia stood near a boat. I stumbled

forward, the wind battering me and whipping the strands of my hair into my face. It hadn't yet started to rain, but I could feel moisture in the heavy air.

"What will I look like?" I repeated as I neared.

Her gown billowed in the gale winds but her golden hair barely moved.

"You will look much like you do now. Hair flying and eyes burning bright. Only, you will be covered with giant flames."

That didn't sound so bad.

"And the rest?"

"In the boat." She motioned to the vessel the waves were trying their hardest to pull back out into open waters.

I stared at the boat that had carried me most of the way to the isle. The plug was once again in place, and both oars waited for me. My bag, which had held my change of clothes, lay ripped and empty in the bottom of the boat. There was no salt. No weapons. And, the oracle wanted me to head out into storm-tossed waters just before sunset.

Our eyes met, and she smiled slowly.

"In you go, Megan. Once you're in the water, we'll both get what we want."

"You want me dead." I said it without thinking, but I knew I was right when she smiled wider.

"Stay here with me and never learn the truth, or get in the boat and take your chances with the open waters."

"Not much of a choice," I said.

"But it's still a choice. And one only you can decide."

Pushing back my hair, I stepped into the boat. It rocked under me then jerked forward. I looked back at Lucia, who was pushing me into the crashing waves.

"The answer," I yelled over the noise.

"Row, Megan. And, I will keep my word."

I started rowing, getting drenched quickly with the first wave that hit the bow.

Lucia's voice carried to me as I put distance between the shore and the boat.

"Controlling your temper is like asking a fish not to swim. You were born to be angry. There is no controlling it. Those who've told you otherwise have been lying to you."

Adira. The Quills. The Council. They'd all lied to me. Everything I'd been told to do. All the tests. Lies. Why? They were keeping my mark from me based on my inability to control my rage. Did that mean I would never get my mark? That I would be forever trapped in Uttira?

I saw red. And through that color-stamped haze of emotion, I also saw Lucia change. Her beautiful face melted away to reveal the sleek flat head of a snake. Her body elongated, and her arms and legs disappeared.

Suddenly, I understood what she really meant when she said we'd both get what we wanted once I was in the water. She had given me my answer, and now she was going to get what she'd wanted all along. A meal.

I pulled hard on the oars and ignored the icy water hitting my back. Nothing mattered but rowing as fast as I could. My life depended on it.

CHAPTER NINETEEN

I watched Lucia slither forward on her belly and enter the foamy surf.

The intent to kill danced in the reflective silver of her eyes. So, why wasn't I angry? Where the hell was my fury temper?

"Of all the times to conveniently disappear, now isn't one of them. A make out session with Oanen? Yes. Two minutes from being sushi? No."

The oracle opened her mouth wide and tested the air with her forked tongue. Then, she ducked under an incoming wave and started in my direction, her body zigzagging smoothly through the turbulent water.

I shivered again and rowed harder, keeping my seat by bracing my feet against the next one. The oars groaned under the strain of my effort to move faster.

"I am not going to be eaten by a twenty-foot snake." Yet, the waves fought me, reducing the forward thrust of each stroke.

Lucia drew closer.

I lifted the oars out of the water and took one from its holder, ready to use it as a weapon. If beating her with it didn't work, I'd shove it down her throat.

At the last moment, her head dipped under the water. The boat lurched forward, away from the island with increasing speed. The swells grew bigger, nearly unseating me as the boat powered over them. I set the oar down and gripped the sides of the boat instead, wondering what Lucia was doing. Behind the boat, the island rapidly grew smaller.

Just before it vanished into the dark haze of the horizon, Lucia stopped pushing. I released my hold on the boat and scrambled to pick up the oar once more.

Lucia's large, wet body flew out of the water and landed in the boat with me. Her tail pinning the oar in place, she opened her mouth. I reacted without thought and punched her in her exposed throat. She jerked back and hissed at me.

"What's wrong?" I taunted. "Don't like it when your food fights back?"

She shifted to her human form, white gown in place and weirdly dry. With a hand covering her throat, she scowled at me.

"As much as I desire to discover the taste of young fury, I'm not yet ready for a journey to the underworld. So, I'll bait my trap like they baited theirs."

"What?" I asked.

"It was no accident you made it to my island, an island hidden by magic even from the land and air creatures here. You made a mermaid mad by stealing her sweet human, and she thought by sending you to me, I would take care of her problem. Usually, I would be inclined to help if it fills my belly. But, I'm not foolish enough to do anything that might gain the attention of the gods."

"What do you mean?" I asked. "Aren't they dead or sleeping or something?"

"Or something," Lucia answered, shifting her attention to the waves around us. She picked up the oar and put it back in its place. When she turned her eyes to me, the pupils were wide and reflective again.

"Row, Megan."

"Why?"

"As I've said, I'm inclined to do things that will help fill my belly. I do very much enjoy the taste of mermaid."

That Lucia wanted to use me as bait to catch another mermaid for dinner was now very clear. But, what would happen to me once she got her mermaid?

I stared at her for a moment, considering my options. Nothing had really changed. I still needed to get back before dark.

Exhaling slowly, I gripped the oars and struggled to make more progress away from the island. The further I got, the warmer I became. I should have felt relief because I was returning back to my version of normal, but there was still so much wrong with my current situation. That I was losing daylight and not gaining much distance didn't worry me as much as what would happen when I lost sight of the island. There was no sun, and I had no GPS to guide me.

As I rhythmically pulled at the water, the sky lightened briefly. Then, the first snowflake fell.

"Shit," I swore under my breath.

Lucia's gaze shifted from the water to the sky, and she smiled.

"Be a good girl and go for a swim," she said softly.

Before I could tell her to go to hell, she shifted forms again. Her tail lashed out and hit me hard across my back.

There was no stopping my graceless topple from the boat. The freezing water slammed into me face-first. Any heat that I generated was ripped from me just as quickly as it appeared. The choppy waves kept me under and rolled me several times, disorientating me. When I opened my eyes, it took a moment for me to focus in the murk. Churned up by the storm, bits of weed and debris floated here and there in an otherwise still, underwater world.

I kicked hard toward the frothing of motion above me, and my head finally broke through the surface. Gulping a breath, I looked around for the boat and spotted it several yards away. Lucia was nowhere in sight. I shuddered at the thought of her slithering in the water with me as I started toward the boat.

Waves washed over my head as I swam. I tried not to think about Lucia or how cold the water was or how to get back to the shore. Instead, I focused on my current goal. I just needed to get in the boat. Another wave hit me. It knocked me under water and rolled me once.

Again needing to find my way back to the surface, I opened my eyes and almost choked at the face staring back at me. The mermaid smiled. Lightning fast, she snagged my hair and started towing me deeper.

My temper flickered then ignited, and water bubbled off of me in a rush. The mermaid didn't notice until I grabbed her arm. She squealed, the sound hurting my ears even underwater. With her free hand, she swiped at me, just missing my face with her claws. I released her and watched her dart away into the surrounding darkness before I kicked my way to the surface.

I breathed in deeply and looked for the boat again. Any progress I'd made in my first attempt to reach it had been lost. Diving under the water this time, I swam hard. The heat from the run-in with the mermaid stayed with me until I surfaced again. I shivered slightly as I focused on the boat, which was much closer this time. Going under once more, I powered my way toward my reprieve from the stupid lake filled with asshole creatures that all wanted to eat me.

When I surfaced, the boat was right there. I closed my hand over the side in relief. Before I could pull myself up, though, something pried my fingers off. Unprepared for the loss of support, I went under again. This time, there were more faces around me. At least a dozen mermaids.

They darted my way, teeth flashing. Something fell into the water. The explosion of white bubbles made it impossible to see what, but I suddenly knew. Lucia hadn't left the boat. She'd been hiding, waiting for her bait to work.

I kicked for the surface, the need to get out of the water that very second overriding everything else. The mermaids not near the churning bubbles grabbed for me. I managed to kick one in the side, but another one bit my arm. My breath left me in a scream of rage. The water started bubbling off of me again, and the mermaids trying to keep me under darted away.

Kicking toward the surface, I grabbed for the boat but it moved just out of reach. I ducked under the next wave and looked around. Lucia bolted past me, hot on a mermaid's tail. Her abrupt appearance sent the mermaids who held the boat scattering. I swam hard for the vessel, staying under water until the last moment. Once more I took hold of the rim and tried to haul myself over the edge.

With a grunt I fell into the bottom of the boat. Laying there, I listened to the waves and caught my breath. My arm ached. I lifted it and studied the tiny punctures that formed a wide crescent. Dark green goo oozed from it already.

"We're not done yet," a voice yelled.

The boat tilted sharply to the side.

I snarled, sat up, and grabbed an oar ready to beat back the finned bitch trying to return me to the lake. The water erupted upward, dousing me yet again. Not that I paid much attention to that as I dropped the oar and wildly grabbed for the side of the boat to keep from falling out.

Lucia's body soared out of the water, sailing overhead. I tracked her progress, slack jawed at the sight of the mermaid she had by the tail. The mermaid squealed and thrashed as they slammed into the water on the other side of the boat.

A wave jostled the boat, snapping me from my stunned slouch against the seat. I grabbed up the oar, slammed it into place and started rowing. I no longer had any sense of where I was. It didn't matter. I just knew I needed to get away from the fighting before I went in again. My arms and legs ached; and outside of the water, away from the mermaids, my fury temper wasn't keeping me warm enough. I couldn't seem to stop shivering, and I doubted it had anything to do with the snow, now falling in earnest, or the fading light. Glancing at the bites on my arm, I forced myself to row harder.

My hair froze to my head as I strained.

Several times, I saw Lucia's body rise only to disappear again. When something burst from the surface near the end of the boat, I thought it was her. Instead, a mermaid landed on the seat in front of me. She immediately shifted from fins to legs, hissed at me, then stared out at the waves.

One minute the mermaid sat there, the next Lucia exploded out of the water, snatched up the girl, and swallowed her whole before plunging back into the depths of the lake.

I forgot to row as I stared at the space where the oracle had disappeared.

"That should have been you," a familiar voice said.

The boat tipped and, unprepared, I went over the side again. I barely felt the cold as the lake swallowed me whole. I kicked hard toward the surface, tired and pissed. My head bobbed through a wave, and I looked around for the boat. It rocked nearby.

Before I could start in that direction, Lucia's head surfaced near mine. She circled me twice, her oddly bulging body skimming the surface. I didn't miss the way her middle wiggled from the inside. Revulsion filled me but no anger. What was wrong with me? How could the mermaids be wicked, but not the mermaid-eating oracle?

Lucia stopped scanning the water and focused on me.

"Such a tasty looking bit, you are. So pale with pretty blue lips. You're getting tired." Her tongue flicked out.

"What happened to not angering the gods?" I asked.

She chuckled.

"Smart little fledgling. That hasn't changed. But there are a few mermaids who might be willing to risk that." She looked out over the water. I followed her gaze and saw several heads watching us.

"This has been fun, my sweet treats," Lucia said. "We'll need to do it again soon." The mermaids hissed at her. "If you happen to kill Megan before sunrise, bring her to me. I wouldn't mind a taste. In fact, I might even reward the one who brings her to me."

She dove under the water, disappearing from sight.

The mermaids and I stared at each other for a moment. They went under. I bolted for the boat.

Within seconds, someone grabbed my ankle and pulled me beneath the surface. I kicked hard and connected with a body part. A squeal rang out. A hand grabbed my bitten arm. Fingers caught my hair. Claws raked my side, setting paths of fire in the skin over my ribs.

I could barely think through the pain as another blazing trail ignited over my thigh. My struggles to get free lost their strength and slowed. I was angry. But, I was so tired too.

Hands gripped my head, turning me and forcing my attention to the wide eyes only inches away from mine. The familiar face smiled.

"You're mine," she said. Her grip tightened as she tugged me upward. The mermaids holding my arms and legs didn't let go but followed as Merbitch and I broke through to the surface.

"What's wrong, Megan?" she asked. "Where are your threats to boil us alive now?"

233

"Go to hell," I said. My tone lacked its usual bite, and I knew I was in serious trouble.

"You wish. I'm going to enjoy this."

"Spare me your villain monologue and just do what you need to do."

She hissed at me and slashed a claw down my neck. I grunted at the burn.

"Do you know what that venomous snake eats when we don't bring her a human? Us! Our brothers and sisters."

"Do you think I care or that I'll give you pity after you tried to feed me to her? Feed Ashlyn to her? You really are stupid."

She pulled her hand back, looking pissed enough to tear my face off as she swung forward. Before her claws could touch me, an eagle's cry split the air.

My pulse jumped in hope and fear. Before Merbitch could dive under, she was ripped out of the water. I looked up in time to see her dangling from Oanen's talons. She screamed and thrashed as he climbed higher into the sky.

A hand locked around my ankle.

"Oan—"

Water closed over my head once more. A second later, a very large and very pissed griffin plunged into the water. The mermaid holding me squealed and tried to flee, but Oanen's beak caught her fin and ripped it clean off.

I grinned slightly, feeling vindicated as I slowly drifted toward the surface. I bobbed there, my blinks becoming slower as I waited for Oanen to emerge. He did several moments later in a shower of water with a mermaid by her tail. He flung his head to the side, and I watched her go flying.

He turned toward me, his golden gaze sweeping my face. I wrapped my arms around his neck and held him, my fear of hurting him gone. I had no heat left in me.

"I am so glad you're here," I said. "Rowing sucks."

His beak nuzzled my hair for a moment before he started to bump me. He didn't quit until I floated on my back.

"You could have just said, 'float' you know," I mumbled.

He jumped out of the water, hovering above me. His talons circled my torso, and with the heavy beat of his wings echoing around us, he pulled me from the waves. I wrapped my hand around his leg and closed my eyes.

Vaguely, I knew there were things I should have been doing, like wondering why I wasn't burning Oanen or asking how he'd found me; but my brain felt too fuzzy to focus. Instead of trying to force my mind to work, I focused on nothing.

Wind and pelting flakes of snow buffeted my face. That stinging burn was nothing compared to the agony growing inside of me. A shudder coursed through my body, and Oanen cried out.

"I'm fine," I said. "I'm just sick of smelling like fish. Take me home, bird boy."

I'd never felt so tired before in my life. As much as I wanted to blame it on all the swimming and rowing, I couldn't. Pain ate at me from the inside. Not wanting to worry Oanen, I forced myself to relax as much as I could in his hold. I focused on the steady thump of his wings, the howl of the wind, and the crash of the waves. It didn't help. Tracing the feathers under my fingers did. A little.

My heart ached with how much I'd missed him. I

couldn't wait to get back home, shower, and snuggle under a tower of blankets with Oanen wrapped around me. The thought of being warm sent another shiver through me.

He made another sound, but I didn't have it in me to comfort him.

My fingers gave a final stroke to his ankle feathers then stilled. The oozing mermaid bites and cuts were sapping me of everything. Only, this time, I wasn't burning up. I was growing colder. So cold, in fact, that after a few minutes, my shivers stopped. I knew that wasn't good. But, sleep pulled at me, and the agony of my injuries began to fade. I sighed, ready to give into the exhaustion.

Oanen's eagle scream jolted through me, and I opened my eyes to see the shoreline and Eliana's car illuminated by the glow of her headlights. Home.

I exhaled heavily and closed my eyes again, dangling loosely in Oanen's grip. My back gently touched ground.

A moment later, Oanen's warm arms wrapped around me.

"Do you have a blanket?" he said. "Anything. She's so cold."

"Cold?" Eliana said, sounding worried. A hand brushed my forehead. "No. We didn't bring a blanket. Here. Take my jacket."

Material covered my torso. It didn't help.

"Megan, open your eyes," Oanen said.

I wanted to. I just didn't have the energy.

His lips pressed against my forehead then my temple, leaving little patches of heat that too quickly faded.

"You're scaring me," he said softly. "I can hear the beat of your heart. But, it's too slow, and I can't feel anything.

Please, Megan. Open those pretty eyes." His hold on me tightened.

My heart ached for Oanen. I tried harder to open my eyes. To move my hand and stroke his hair. I had nothing left. What was wrong with me? I'd never felt sick in my life, but now…it felt like I was dying.

CHAPTER TWENTY

"PLEASE, MEGAN," OANEN WHISPERED AGAIN. "GET MAD. You need to warm up. Don't leave me." His voice broke on those last words.

Held tightly against his chest, I wished I could hold him in return. Touch him. Talk to him. Now was my chance. I was cold enough that I could actually do all the things I wanted to do without hurting him. Instead of moving though, I just lay there, trapped inside of myself.

He pulled away and touched his lips to mine. The light press of heat against my cold skin started a flutter in my belly.

When his lips left me a moment later, I wanted to beg for him to come back.

"Don't stop," Eliana said. I heard her shuffle closer.

"What?" Oanen asked.

"I could feel something from her. It was faint but there. Kiss her again."

His hand cupped my face.

"Come on, Megan," he said softly.

My fingers twitched at the feel of his mouth brushing gently over mine. The warmth of his exhale washed over my face as his fingers traced the curve of my cheek. Heat ignited in my stomach, hard and fast. It burned through me, setting each cut and bite ablaze. But there wasn't any pain, only the taste of Oanen.

Determined not to waste my chance, I lifted my hands and threaded my fingers through his hair. With a relief-torn sound, he deepened the kiss. The first touch of his tongue to mine felt like it set fire to my skin. I groaned and slid my hands from his hair to his bare chest. I'd been so hungry for him. For the feel of his arms around me. I wanted to hold on and never let go. I wanted him over me. In me.

A hand slapped down on the top of my head, cooling all my Oanen-centered thoughts.

I jerked back and looked up into his golden eyes. The heat I saw reflected in his gaze made my insides curl with delight. However, the sparks of passion that continued to pop and flare inside of me, couldn't seem to ignite again.

"Oanen," Eliana said, sounding strange, "your eyebrows just grew back. Go stand by the car."

He pulled away from me with obvious reluctance, and I hungrily watched his retreating backside.

"And put some clothes on," Eliana added.

I tilted my head up at her and noted her pure black eyes as she watched Oanen follow her orders.

"Miss me, monkey?" I asked.

Her gaze dipped to me.

"I'm so mad at you. Don't ever make me do this again." She gave my hair a slight tug, making it clear what she never wanted to do again, and lifted her hand.

"I thought you liked the taste of fury," I said, batting my lashes at her.

"Fury. Not lust."

"Liar," Oanen said from near the car.

I glanced his way, and all the passion I had for him slammed back into me. Only this time, it didn't feel so good. The heat flared to life in the wounds, burning them with molten pain. I made a sound, and Eliana reached for me.

"Don't," I managed to say. "Not this time."

Oanen took several steps in my direction, and I held up my hand.

"No. I'll be okay."

I wasn't sure I would be, though. I couldn't remember it hurting so much the last time I'd healed. Everything ached. Pain radiated through me. Anger swiftly followed. None of this needed to happen.

"Talk to me, Megan," Oanen said. "What's wrong?"

"I'm hurt, and I'm pissed," I said.

"Hurt? Where?"

I pulled back the sleeve of my steaming shirt to expose the mermaid bite. Green sludge dripped from my skin to the melting snow beneath me.

"None of this needed to happen," I said, echoing my earlier thought. "Oanen leaving to search for my mom. My trip to the damn lake for the oracle. Every single bite and scrape. It's all the result of adult bullshit."

Another intense stab of pain bolted through me. I clenched my teeth against the need to cry out and waited for it to pass.

"If my mom hadn't taken off," I said when I could

speak, "or if anyone in this place would just tell the truth for once—"

The next piercing shard of agony tore a scream from me. The smell of something burning clogged my nose as I struggled to inhale.

"That's right. Breathe, Megan," Oanen said. "Focus on me. On the sound of my voice."

I opened my eyes, which I hadn't realized I'd closed, and found Oanen squatted down a few yards from me. His face was red and beaded with sweat. Just behind him, Eliana stood with wide eyes as she stared at me.

"Sweet Jesus," she said softly.

Panting with pain, I looked down at myself. Flames licked my skin around the bite, burning away my sleeve.

Was this how I healed?

Before that thought fully settled in my mind, the fire spread, racing up my arm. I looked at Oanen, panic coursing through me as quickly as the flames were consuming me.

"You're okay, Megan," he said. "It's not burning you."

"The hell it isn't! It hurts like a bitch."

"Look at your skin. You're fine."

I looked down again, seeing he was right. Why was it hurting then? I groaned again as the inferno inside of me burst outward. The roar of flames filled my ears, and my skin tightened to the point it felt like it would split.

Then it all stopped. I fell to my knees, panting and tired and wondering at what point I'd gotten to my feet.

"She's okay, Oanen. Why don't you get your shirt?"

I lifted my head to look at the pair. Eliana held Oanen's arm to keep him from coming toward me. His eyes met mine, and my heart melted at the worry I saw there.

"I'm okay," I said.

"Go get her your shirt," Eliana said, nudging him toward her car. "She needs a minute."

I frowned and looked down to see how much damage I'd caused my clothes. My mouth dropped open. I wasn't wearing a thing. Crossing an arm over my boobs and shielding my nethers with a hand, I looked up again. Oanen had already turned around on his way to the car.

Eliana gave me a sheepish smile.

"Looks like you might need to start stashing clothes, too," she said.

"I really hope that kind of thing will not be a regular occurrence," I said, carefully getting to my feet. The now exposed sand beneath me had melted into an irregular sheet of glass.

"It looked like it might be."

"What do you mean?"

She shrugged slightly and lifted the phone she held, turning it so I could see the picture she'd taken. I was floating in the air, arms flung wide, consumed in an inferno of flames. My mouth was open, and my head flung back. Everything about me was on fire. Even my hair. I squinted and stepped closer, trying to ignore the fact that I was completely exposed in the picture.

"What's that behind me?" I asked as I stared at the twin flames that extended from either side of me.

"It looks like small wings."

"Can my life get any worse? I'm going to kill that oracle."

"Why?"

Before I could answer, Oanen approached with a shirt held loosely in his hands. The heated look in his eyes made my insides flare with warmth again.

"Cool it, you two," Eliana said. "Oanen, turn around. Megan, keep talking."

Oanen winked at me as he tossed the shirt over then gave us his back. I quickly tugged the covering on over my head.

"The oracle didn't say a thing about wings. She also told me that there was no way to control my temper and that Adira and the Council have been lying to me."

"Hmm," Eliana said, looking off toward the lake.

Oanen turned around and tugged me into his arms while she was distracted.

"Don't ever scare me like that again," he said against my hair.

"Not sure I can promise that. I think Eliana's right, and flames might be another superpower for me."

"I wasn't talking about the flames. Why didn't you wait for me?"

"Because I wanted to be able to hug you without turning you into a piece of extra crispy when you got back. I don't want to hurt you anymore."

"I don't think you will. I'm holding you now, and I'm fine."

I looked up at his red face and made a sound of doubt.

"This is because I was too close when you exploded. You're not too hot now."

I lifted up to my toes and kissed him hard. He kissed me back. For several long moments, there was nothing but me and Oanen and what we felt for each other. I basked in the ability to kiss him and touch him like I wanted.

Distantly, I heard Eliana clear her throat.

"I think you can safely conclude you're in control of yourself now," Eliana called.

I pulled back to see Oanen's golden eyes. He still had all of his facial hair. I grinned. He threaded his fingers through mine and gave me a tender look.

"Since we know you won't hurt me anymore, how about we promise to stick together from now on?" he said. "No more trying to break up with me."

"I think I can manage that." My smile faded as my temper spiked. "What is up with everyone lying in this dump?"

"The Council?" Oanen asked.

"No, the oracle. She said that there was no controlling my temper. I just hugged you without setting you on fire."

"I think the oracle told you the truth, Megan," Eliana said, standing by the car. When I focused on her, I noticed the car's paint had bubbled.

"Holy shit," I said, looking at what I'd done.

"Yeah, no more monkey hugs for you when you're mad," Eliana said.

"No kidding. Now, why do you think she told the truth?"

"Because if there was someone wicked nearby, I don't think you'd be able to control your temper. That you're not burning Oanen or me accidently means you're in control of your power. I think you can control your power, but not your anger. Your anger is what helps you identify the wicked."

"That's splitting hairs. I have no doubt she purposely misled me. You know what the most frustrating part is? By my definition, she was wicked, yet I didn't get fury angry at her."

"Why do you think she was wicked?" Eliana asked.

"She's been eating mermaids. A lot of them. And, I saw her do it."

"There's no rule that says she can't eat mermaids or other creatures," Oanen said. "Only that we can't consume human flesh."

"She did say she always tried to follow the rules," I said, thinking things through. "That whole trip was a complete waste then. She didn't tell me anything that would help me."

My temper jumped a bit, and I quickly looked down at our joined hands. His thumb stroked over my skin, no hint of red appearing. I wasn't generating any external heat.

"Not a waste," Oanen said, drawing my attention. "Not if you really can control your powers now."

"I think we should test it," Eliana said.

"How?"

She grinned widely.

"Let's go to the Roost."

"I DON'T LIKE THIS," I said, looking at the Roost's red doors through the passenger window.

"Me, neither," Oanen said.

"Stop being babies," Eliana said from the back seat.

"This is the best way to test if Megan's fixed, and you both know it."

I wanted to deny I was ever broken, but given the number of times I'd burned Oanen, I couldn't.

"Fine. Let's just get this done."

I opened my door and stood, wincing at the cold air whirling around my bare legs. Oanen's t-shirt extended past my butt by a meager three inches. While I'd wanted to go home and change first, Eliana had argued that showing up in nothing but a t-shirt would be more likely to illicit wicked ideas from the patrons.

"I swear, if anyone sees my butt, I'm going to be so mad."

"Good. That's the point," Eliana said as she got out to stand by me.

"Mad at you," I clarified.

She smiled, clearly not worried about my temper. The driver's side door opened, and I looked back at Oanen.

"Are you sure you don't want to wait in the car?" I asked.

"Together, remember?"

I nodded and started for the entrance. As usual, music already thumped from inside even though it was barely six.

The light dusting of new snow covering the sidewalk swirled around my feet as I opened the door. Warm air enveloped me, but I didn't get a chance to enjoy it.

A tingle of annoyance immediately traced down my spine. Without pausing, I strode in and pushed my way through the dancers toward the back of the room. A few of the guys on the floor paused to look at me. I could feel the nudge of their wickedness as they took in the sight of my breasts barely concealed by Oanen's thin t-shirt. That wickedness only inflated when they saw I wasn't wearing pants. However, their thoughts were pure in comparison to what I felt coming from the back of the club.

Instead of trying to calm down or run away, I opened myself to my temper. Details flooded my mind. Things I shouldn't know. Like my temper was flaring because Eras was harassing Kelsey and Zoe, again. But, that wasn't the sole cause. Something else was poking at me. Something he'd done in the past that I couldn't see for myself in the present.

I broke through the dancing crowd and found Eras and his friends sitting at the back table with Kelsey and Zoe, who were both clutching their books and keeping their heads down.

"Come on, girls," Eras said in a seductive voice. "You don't need to look at me. No one else needs to know. It'll be between us. Just nod. I'll reach under the table and have you shaking with need in seconds. It'll feel amazing. I promise."

"Not nearly as amazing as this," I said, my voice echoing with my fury power. "Eras Amadeus Aeccin, confess your sins."

Eras's mouth fell slack as he turned to look at me. The boys at the table with him quickly scrambled away.

Kelsey and Zoe's heads jerked up. They stared at me with wide eyes, both looking like they were about to cry. Eliana quickly stepped around me and slid into the booth to comfort them.

"Don't make me repeat myself, Eras," I said.

His mouth snapped shut.

"I wasn't breaking any rules, Fury. There's no reason for you to attack me."

"Oh, but there is. Something you did in your past. Something that did break the rules." The heat inside me intensified. I didn't fight it as I stepped closer to him and leaned down.

"Confess."

The soft word set off a blubbering confession about some petty theft, voyeurism (which I highly doubted was a crime), and vandalism. The last one made me scowl as he detailed how he'd smashed my window and seduced a mermaid into scratching my paint.

"You are guilty of wickedness," I said, grabbing Eras by the collar of his polo shirt and hauling him from the booth. The boy was a sobbing mess.

"Continue on this course, and you are guaranteed a spot in Hell's hall. Make amends and cleanse your slate."

"I'll make amends. I promise. Just tell me what to do."

His eagerness and complete sincerity calmed my temper.

"Uttira needs a library. Help build it."

He nodded frantically, and I let go of his shirt. He thumped to the ground and dashed for the door. Only after the fact, did I realize what I'd just done. I'd controlled my power by letting my temper go. I'd also just exposed the hell out of my backside.

I turned to face the room.

"Did anyone here see my butt just now?"

Every single head started to shake.

"Remember, lies are wicked," I said with a frown.

Half the people nervously raised their hands.

"Can you reach over the table again?" Fenris shouted from within the crowd. "I didn't get a good look. Oanen got in the way."

I glanced at Oanen, who looked mad enough to skin a dog.

"How about you and I head home," I said softly.

Before he could say anything, a portal appeared beside us and Adira stepped out.

"Oanen has other obligations tonight, Megan," she said. "As do you."

"Oh? And what might our obligations be?" I asked, arching a brow.

"The Council would like Oanen to fly to the Goose and Gizzard in New York on official business, and I have two more recruits for you to verify."

I looked at Kelsey and Zoe, who were still pale. Although some of the color loss could be blamed on Eras, I knew most of it was due to me.

"I'm sorry, guys," I said.

"No, we're cool," Kelsey said. "We didn't see anything."

I started to grin, but my temper flared hot and fast, the only warning I had to turn and grab Adira's wrist before she could touch my shoulder. I let all the anger Adira and the Council had caused to burn in my eyes.

When she saw the flames there, she flinched and paled.

"I warned you not to toy with me, Adira. Don't ever try to teleport me without my permission again. Do we understand each other?"

"Yes. Perfectly. With your permission, I would like to teleport all three of us to the Quills' for an overdue meeting."

"No. Oanen has been gone for days. He's not doing anything tonight but spending time with me. And, I'm not verifying another recruit for you ever again. Uttira needs to fix its educational process before putting more fish in the fish bowl. Are we clear?"

"Yes. Please come see us first thing in the morning."

I rolled my eyes.

"I'll see you when it's convenient to me. Now, stop pushing."

She gave a single nod then disappeared.

Eliana's phone immediately buzzed. She looked at it with a frown.

"What?" I asked.

"It's from Adira, and it's for Oanen. She says to keep a close eye on Megan tonight."

I smiled widely. Adira had just confirmed what I'd suspected the moment she'd paled. The Council knew they could no longer control me. I was free. Almost.

Oanen stepped close and wrapped his arms around my waist. He pressed his lips to my temple in a brief kiss and looked at Eliana.

"I already planned to keep a very close eye on her. Tonight and every night after."

CHAPTER TWENTY-ONE

I SCRUBBED MY HAIR A SECOND TIME BEFORE ADDING conditioner. At my feet, bits of seaweed swirled near the drain.

"I hate mermaids," I called loud enough for Oanen to hear. He probably would have heard without me yelling, but I wanted the volume to convey the loathing I felt.

"Lakes too!"

I finished up in the shower and quickly dressed. When I joined him in the kitchen, he was leaning against the counter, waiting for me.

"So a moonlit ride in a gondola is out?"

"Since gondolas are usually found in Italy, no. I'd suffer some water for that to happen. But more swimming in Lake Uttira? No way."

He pushed away from the counter and stalked toward me. My stomach fluttered wildly, but nothing started burning. I still couldn't believe that I was okay.

He snagged the edge of my shirt and slowly reeled me into his arms.

"Are we done fighting this, now?"

"You were never fighting it," I said with a small smile.

"Stubborn fury, just answer the question."

I grinned and stood on my toes to kiss him lightly.

"I'm done fighting what's happening between us."

"Good." He released me then tugged me toward the table where he had sandwiches waiting for us. A brownie sat on my plate, too.

"I'm so hungry," I said. I sat and took a huge bite, moaning at the taste of mayonnaise and turkey.

"Thought you might be." His lips twitched as he watched me swallow. "That brownie is from Michigan, which is where I was when Eliana called me."

I wrinkled my nose and squinted at him.

"Is this where you lecture me again?"

"Nope." He picked up his sandwich and took a bite.

I could see he wanted to say more and waited for him to finish chewing. He didn't leave me waiting long.

"I'm too smart to annoy a fury with lectures."

"I'm going to remember that."

"I bet you will. I'm sorry I didn't find your mom," he said, changing the subject. "I'll look again when I go to New York."

"We'll look," I said after finishing another bite.

He frowned at me.

"Did you already forget our promise?" I asked. "Together from now on. Remember?"

"That might be a problem when I need to leave for Council matters."

I grinned. "I don't think so. First, there's no longer any reason for the Council to keep me trapped here. I'm not burning you every time we touch now, and I didn't beat Eras tonight even though I was angry. That means I have control. I just have to tell Adira tomorrow. Second, the Council doesn't own you. You're the one who told me not to be a cog in their wheel of lies."

"I don't recall saying wheel of lies," he said, the corner of his mouth twitching.

"It was implied. Regardless, they don't own you, right? So, until I get my mark, we'll stick together. And once I have my mark, if you choose to continue to help the Council, I'll go also. If we're lucky, we'll run into my mom at some point."

"You still want to find her?" he asked.

"Yeah. I want to know why she couldn't have spent five minutes explaining things to me instead of just bailing."

After we finished up our late dinner, we went to the living room where we watched TV together. Oanen held me the whole time, his fingers traveling the length of my arm. I stopped watching several times to turn my head and kiss him. Each time ended with me breathless and wanting more. But, no fire. No burns.

I STARED OUT AT THE QUILLS' large house, not looking forward to our meeting.

"We can go do something else," Oanen said.

I laughed lightly and shook my head.

"There's nothing else to do in this town at eight in the morning."

"We could go back to bed."

I turned to him and arched my brow. We spent the night comfortably sleeping in each other's arms. It'd been the best night's sleep I'd had in ages. The kisses he'd trailed along my neck to wake me had been amazing, too.

"I like this new you," he said. "I know when you're thinking about me. Your eyes start glowing light orange."

"How do you know I wasn't getting mad at you?"

"They start glowing a deeper orange when you're angry."

I rolled my eyes and shook my head at him.

"As much as I want to have a repeat of last night, I also want to get this done." I glanced at the house again. "You won't try to stop me, right?"

"No. I'll support whatever decisions you make in there. Even against my parents. I trust you, Megan."

"All right. Let's do this."

We got out and walked the snow-covered path. As usual, his mom opened the door before we reached it.

"Good morning you two," she said with a wide smile.

I frowned at her barely contained joy, not trusting it.

"I changed my mind. Let's leave," I said softly, threading my fingers through Oanen's.

A look of hurt crossed Mrs. Quill's face.

"I know these past few weeks have been a struggle for you—"

"No thanks to the Council and Adira," I said.

"—but I want you to know, I couldn't be happier with Oanen's choice in a mate."

Oh, sure. Now, she was happy.

Oanen's fingers squeezed mine lightly, and I knew I needed to be gracious for his sake.

"Thanks." That was as gracious as she was getting from me after trying to keep us apart.

She smiled and stepped aside to let us in.

"We're meeting in the study," she said.

Oanen and I walked the familiar path. When we entered, I was surprised to see several people already there. While I recognized Fenris' dad, Mr. Quill, and Adira, the rest were new to me.

"Thank you for coming, Megan," Adira said, turning toward me. "With your permission, my sister and I would like to lay our hands on you."

I glanced at Oanen, wondering what the hell was going on. The amused glint in his eyes and encouraging nod had me agreeing. He released my hand and took a few steps back.

Mrs. Quill touched one shoulder and Adira the other. Both said several soft words I couldn't understand. A flare of pain scorched the inside of my wrist, and I jerked back from their hold. Lifting my arm, I saw the small, umber mark of Mantirum decorating my skin.

"Congratulations, Megan," Adira said.

"I don't understand. I thought there was a whole process to ensure I was ready. Questions that the Council needed to ask me."

"The process is different for each candidate. You proved your control last night. We saw no reason to delay giving you the mark. We do ask that you leave Uttira as soon as possible."

That got my attention.

"What? Are you serious? First you're hell-bent on keeping me here, and now you're kicking me out?"

"Yes," Adira said. "That's the condition of your mark. Having a mature fury inside Uttira is dangerous to the young still trying to learn the rules of our world. We want to ensure they have a chance to learn to do what's right before being punished for any mistakes made in ignorance. Oanen, you're welcome back any time, of course."

My temper flared, and the orange glow from my eyes reflected on Adira's skin.

"No," I said firmly. Everyone watched me, waiting. I could feel their fear. Of me.

"I will go, but I will return as I choose. And, I will punish the wicked as I see fit. If you truly want to protect your young, set better examples and start teaching them the rules from the moment they are born. Stop with the ridiculous classes in the Academy. Start teaching them their history and why they need to toe the line. And let them know, when they break the rules, there are bigger consequences than banishment from Uttira. I'll drag them to hell."

Raiden dipped his head.

"Yes, Fury."

All the rest followed suit and said the same.

Oanen took my hand again, reclaiming my attention.

"Want to hang around for a while, or are you ready to go to New York?"

"I'm ready," I said.

I was finally, truly free.

"IT'S NOT FAIR," Eliana said as she put another item from

the fridge into the cooler. "I mean, it's fair you have your mark; it's not fair that they're making you leave town."

"They're making your mom stay away," I pointed out.

She gave a dry laugh.

"Mom is staying away because I asked her to. She doesn't care what they say. You have your mark; you can come and go as you please. Just stay."

I smiled at her. I would have never survived my time in Uttira without Eliana. I wasn't about to abandon my friend permanently.

"I'll be back," I said.

"Then why are we packing everything up?"

"Because I won't be back soon. It's going to take some time to find my mom."

"What am I supposed to do while you're gone? You are my only friend."

"Not true. You have Ashlyn, now. And Kelsey, Zoe, and Eugene."

She snorted.

"They're afraid of me. They know I'm something but just haven't figured out what yet. When they do, they'll start avoiding me like everyone else."

"Fine. What about Fenris? He knows what you are, and he doesn't ignore you."

She turned and rolled her eyes at me.

"Fenris is the last person I'd want to hang out with."

"I think that would hurt his feelings if he heard you say that," I said. "He's nice."

"He's way too into women. Look at all the trouble he caused because he wouldn't leave you alone."

I stopped trying to stick up for him. He'd need to figure out how to win over Eliana on his own.

"You'll be fine. And if you get bored, you can call me. Or better yet, get your mark so you can come hang out with me in the real world."

She groaned and continued loading things from the fridge to the cooler. My phone buzzed, and I read the text from Oanen.

Hope you're ready. I'll be there in twenty.

"If you got this covered, I'm going to go check over the rest of the house one more time. Oanen will be here in twenty minutes."

"Go for it," she called, her head buried in the fridge.

I walked upstairs and peeked into both rooms. I was leaving the place better than how I'd found it. Well, I was leaving it cleaner anyway. It was just as sad and empty as before, though. How many generations of furies had been dumped here?

"I got everything from the fridge," Eliana called from downstairs. "I'm going to take the cooler out to the car."

I returned to the first floor just as the porch door slammed shut. I checked the bathroom to ensure I had all my toiletries packed then turned around. The dismantled door chime caught my eye and made me smile. It hadn't been easy living here, but it had been an adventure. Several of them, in fact.

Turning, I started toward the kitchen then paused to open the library door. I didn't want the room to get musty if it took a while for me to return. Opening the door somehow knocked over one of the few books on the shelf.

Stepping into the room, I righted the thin tome. My fingers slid over the spine as I read the cover.

The Book of Fury.

Disbelief coursed through me as I plucked the book off the shelf and started to read. It was all there. Everything I needed to know. How to identify the signs of emerging power. How to embrace the anger to control the power. When it was time to leave my child behind so our powers didn't feed off of one another.

I paged through to the end where it talked about the final phase of a fury's growth and found a loose sheet of paper.

I know this probably isn't nearly enough information to answer all the questions you have right now. I'm sorry for that. Here's your great grandmother's address. She'll be waiting for you. Good luck. Call me when it's done.

Love Mom

She'd even written her phone number. I skimmed the letter again. Call when what was done? I looked at the last page of the book and read the words that made a ball form in my stomach.

By the laws of the gods there can be only three furies. Each new generation must tear the oldest generation from her position in order to fully embrace her power.

"Oh, hell no," I said, sitting heavily in the chair.

"Megan?" Eliana said from the doorway. "What's wrong?"

I looked up from the sheet of paper and met my best friend's eyes.

"I think I'm supposed to kill my great grandma."

Thank you for reading *Fury Focused*! The series concludes with *Fury Freed*.
Now available!

AUTHOR'S NOTE

If you've enjoyed Fury Focused, be sure to sign up for my newsletter at https://melissahaag.com/subscribe to find out more about upcoming releases. Want to learn more about Fury Freed, book 3 in Megan's journey? Feel free to check out my Book list section.

Leaving a review is one of the best ways to support an author. Your review might just be the one that persuades more readers to pick up a book you've loved (or hated). And, reviews increase a book's visibility on retailer sites. Please consider leaving a review to help keep my books visible!

Thank you for reading!

Melissa

MORE BOOKS BY MELISSA HAAG

**Judgement of the Six Series
(and Companion Books) in order:**
Hope(less)
*Clay's Hope**
(Mis)fortune
*Emmitt's Treasure**
(Un)wise
*Luke's Dream**
(Un)bidden
*Thomas' Treasure**
(Dis)content
*Carlos' Peace**
*(Sur)real***

optional companion book
**written in dual point of view*

Of Fates and Furies Series
Fury Frayed
Fury Focused
Fury Freed

Other Titles

Touch
Moved
Warwolf
Nephilim